COULD YOU SURVIVE
IN PREHISTORIC TIMES?

AN INTERACTIVE PREHISTORIC ADVENTURE

Content Consultant: Mathew Wedel, PhD
Associate Professor, Department of Anatomy
Western University of Health Sciences
Pomona, California

CAPSTONE PRESS
a capstone imprint

You Choose Books are published by Capstone Press, an imprint of Capstone.
1710 Roe Crest Drive
North Mankato, Minnesota 56003
www.capstonepub.com

Library of Congress Cataloging-in-Publication Data
ISBN: 978-1-4966-9725-7 (paperback)
ISBN: 978-1-9771-5937-3 (eBook PDF)

Summary: Leads readers through prehistoric adventures in which they can choose
what to do and where to go next.

Cover Art
Alessandro Valdrighi (middle and bottom), Juan Calle (top)

Design Elements
Capstone and Shutterstock: Art studio G, DianaFinch, Miceking, Studio Photo
MH, tinkivinki

Editorial Credits
Editor: Mandy Robbins; Designer: Bobbie Nuytten; Media Researcher: Jo Miller;
Production Specialist: Tori Abraham

Printed and bound in China.   005001

TABLE OF CONTENTS

COULD YOU SURVIVE
THE CRETACEOUS PERIOD?

BY ERIC BRAUN
ILLUSTRATED BY ALESSANDRO VALDRIGHI

TABLE OF CONTENTS

INTRODUCTION

YOU are an ordinary kid going about your everyday life. Suddenly, you find yourself in a strange place and a strange time. It's a period from long ago. The world looks different than anything you've ever seen before. Terrifying beasts roam the land. Danger lurks at every turn. Where will you find shelter? How will you get food? Will you ever see your friends and family again? Most importantly of all, can you survive?

Chapter One sets the scene. Then you choose which path to take. Follow the directions at the bottom of each page. The choices you make determine what happens next. After you finish your path, go back and read the others for more adventures.

YOU CHOOSE the path you take through the Cretaceous Period!

Turn the page to begin your adventure.

CHAPTER 1

ONE TOUGH TEST

YOU are taking a test on the Cretaceous Period in science class. The room is silent except for the scratching of pencils. Ms. Turrey is in the back of the room working on a prehistoric terrarium display. Suddenly, you hear some electric pops, and she lets out a startled gasp.

You've always liked Ms. Turrey because she really loves science—and it shows. She's always talking about cool discoveries and cracking science jokes. And she does lots of experiments. Her class is never boring. That's why you don't think much about the noises at first. It's just another one of Ms. Turrey's fun experiments.

But then the room gets humid. A smell comes from the back like mud and leafy plants.

Turn the page.

"Oh my," Ms Turrey says.

You look back. The terrarium contains a model of a Cretaceous Period landscape, complete with plants, toy dinosaurs, and a pool of water representing a sea. For some reason, two big electric cords are attached to the sides of the terrarium. A small gray laptop sits on the table next to it. Its cable has slipped into the fake sea. A gooey liquid sizzles around the computer, eating at the desk. A thick mist wafts from the tank. You drop your pencil.

"Is everything okay?" you ask.

"Please," Ms. Turrey says, "keep working. I'm just going to get the custodian."

She speed walks out. You want to obey her, but your curiosity gets the better of you. You and your best friend, Harriet, go to the now-rumbling tank for a closer look. The mist wraps around you.

"Don't touch anything!" Ms. Turrey calls from the hall. Other students are coming to look too.

Your head suddenly feels strange. Why are you so dizzy? Did the toy Triceratops just look at you? You reach inside the tank to pick it up, and the world spins. You fall back, and when you open your eyes, you're lying on the ground—the muddy ground.

The desks are gone. The tank is gone. Even the walls are gone. Overhead, a pteranodon soars under the sun, dragging its great shadow over you. You don't understand how, but one thing is obvious. You have just been transported to the Cretaceous Period.

To explore a jungle in the Early Cretaceous, turn to page 13.

To wander through a flowery field in the Late Cretaceous, turn to page 43.

To experience the coastline of the sea at the end of the Cretaceous, turn to page 75.

CHAPTER 2

WELCOME TO THE JUNGLE

You wake up on the floor of a forest in a tangle of ferns and other leafy plants. As you open your eyes, you feel a sting on your neck. You slap it, and your hand comes back smeared with blood. The smashed body of a black bug the size of a nickel falls to the dirt by your face. Its legs kick one last time, and it dies.

"What happened?" someone asks.

It's Harriet. She's lying near you in the leaves.

"Ew!" she says, swatting a bug off her hair.

"I can't explain it," you say. "I think we time traveled. It looks like we're in the Cretaceous Period—the Early Cretaceous to be exact."

Turn the page.

"Like on the test," she says.

You're still kneeling on the ground when it begins to rumble. You can feel it through your whole body. Standing up, you look out between the trees and see a herd of huge dinosaurs storming across the plains. Each one is longer than two semitrailers. When they lift their necks, they are taller than your city library—and it's an eight-story building! You know from your science test these are some kind of sauropod. They're not meat eaters, but their sheer size is terrifying. You imagine getting trampled beneath them. There are at least a dozen of them, and each one could use you as a toothpick.

They're heading your way. They are scary, but also fascinating.

To run away, go to the next page.
To hide and watch them, turn to page 17.

"Come on!" you yell.

Harriet follows as you run deeper into the jungle. You leap over a fallen tree. Bugs buzz through the air. A pack of small mammals that you recognize as multituberculates scrambles out of your way and into the brush. They look like rats, but they're the size of house cats.

Finally, the rumbling fades behind you. It's getting dark, and the breeze is chilly. You realize you had better start thinking about shelter. Where is a safe place to sleep? You worry about sleeping on the ground, where any dinosaur or animal could reach you. You look up at the tree in front of you. It is choked with moss, twisty vines, and fern leaves, making the upper branches almost impossible to see into.

"I think we should find a tree where we can spend the night," you say.

Turn the page.

"I'm hungry," Harriet replies.

"Well I don't think we're going to find a cheeseburger tonight. We need to get somewhere safe until morning."

You and Harriet find a tree with a good strong limb and a thick curtain of leaves to keep you hidden. You gather some leaves and vines to keep you as warm as possible, but still you shiver all through the night.

The next morning, Harriet stretches and looks around. She looks exhausted. You know you probably look the same.

"Now about that cheeseburger," Harriet says.

You know she's just kidding. But she is also right—you need food.

To try to catch a multituberculate, turn to page 20.
To eat plants, turn to page 23.

The dinosaurs would crush you like a bug. But they are so beautiful! You've never seen a living thing so large and yet so graceful. No human ever has! You decide to stay in the jungle and watch them.

You and Harriet hide behind a tree and watch. The sauropods lumber toward you. Your heart races, but you hold your position. Then the herd stops and starts eating. One of the incredible beasts prods its long neck in the canopy of trees just above you and pulls off a mouthful of leaves. Its biting and swallowing sounds like a washing machine cycle. Specks of saliva and broken branches fall onto your head. You watch in amazement.

Suddenly, the herd stops eating. They all sense you—you must be mysterious to them. Just as quickly as they came, they leave. The earth rumbles for a few minutes, and then they are gone.

Turn the page.

"That was awesome!" Harriet whispers.

You agree. No matter what you get on your science test, this has been worth it. You are still thinking about the sauropods when you slap an itch on your arm. It's another big black bug. The air buzzes with flying insects, and you wave your hands to shoo them away.

"I hate these bugs!" Harriet says. "Let's get out of the trees. It looks like there aren't as many out in the sunshine."

"I hate them too," you say. "But what about dinosaurs? And other predators? We'd have nowhere to hide out there. We're probably safer in the jungle."

To stay in the jungle, turn to page 27.
To go out onto the plains, turn to page 29.

You think it would be a lot easier to grab some plants than it would be to catch a quick animal. But looking around, it's hard to tell which plants are safe. You know that some plants are toxic to humans. In prehistoric times, maybe all of them are.

"Okay," you say. "Let's give it a shot."

You find a long stick on the ground and sharpen it by scraping it against a rough boulder. Eventually you have a deadly spear. Harriet goes around a stand of shrubs where some of the multituberculates are hiding. She raises her arms and storms toward them.

"Raar!" she yells.

Several of the furry creatures run out of the bushes, right toward you. They flash their sharp little teeth at you, and you jump out of the way.

"Yikes!" you cry.

"Hey," Harriet says. "You have to do better than that!"

"Sorry," you say. "Let's try it again.

Harriet finds another multituberculate and scares it toward you. This time you don't falter. You stab at it with your spear, but you miss. You repeat the process countless more times—the little mammals are everywhere. Finally, you stick one.

"Thank goodness," Harriet says. "I'm starving."

Using your sharpened stick, you skin the creature and pull off the meat.

"Wait," you say. "How can we make a fire? We don't have any matches or anything."

Turn the page.

"Let's just eat it," Harriet says.

She's staring at the meat and licking her lips. You've noticed that she's started acting more and more primitive since you got here. Being trapped in the Cretaceous Period is turning her into some kind of cavewoman.

To eat it raw, turn to page 30.
To try to make a fire, turn to page 34.

You don't want to deal with trying to catch and cook an animal. Gross! Besides, you know a little bit about what is safe to eat in the forest—assuming the prehistoric forest is similar to a modern forest.

"Look for some green balls," you say. "Like tennis balls. They should have nuts inside."

"What about these leaves?" Harriet says, pulling some small bunches from the dirt. "They look like parsley."

"Don't!" you say. "They might be toxic." You scan the trees and find a few green balls. "Here, break these open."

You and Harriet collect more green balls and break them open against a big rock. Soon you are eating a nice meal of nuts. Next, you follow the sloping forest downhill until you find a stream.

Turn the page.

You both take long drinks. The water tastes delicious and fresh.

You freeze when you hear a deafening shriek. Mammals, lizards, snakes, and other creatures are running away from the water back into the forest. Birds rise out of the trees and flee into the sky. What are they afraid of?

When you look up from the water, you get your answer. A dinosaur stands on two giant legs on the other side of the stream, maybe 100 feet away. It towers 20 feet high and has a tall, spiny sail along its back. Its head is longer than your whole body. And when it opens its massive jaws, you see plenty of spiky teeth.

Harriet gasps. "Spinosaurus," she whispers.

"Oh no!" you say. "Those are meat eaters."

"And we are meat," she replies.

Turn the page.

You're terrified! So you do what a terrified person would do. You run. As soon as you start running, the Spinosaurus gives chase. It splashes across the stream. It crashes up the bank on your side. It huffs and barks.

You run faster than you ever thought you could. Harriet is right next to you. But it is no use. You feel the beast's hot breath on your back. You know that your time in the Cretaceous Period has come to an end.

THE END

To follow another path, turn to page 11.
To learn more about the Cretaceous Period, turn to page 105.

"I think we're safer in here," you say. "A few bug bites won't kill us, right?"

"I don't know about that," Harriet says.

She follows you into the jungle anyway. It is an amazing world. A thick tree canopy blots out the sky. Vines, leafy plants, snakes, and little mammals are everywhere. But the bugs are really bad.

"Let's find a stream or river," Harriet says. "If we can find some mud, we can rub it on our skin to keep the bugs off."

You search for over an hour, eventually finding a stream. You each coat your bodies with mud. You even manage to laugh at how silly you look. But it seems to be a little too late. The bug bites you already have are very itchy. You scratch at them with growing intensity.

Turn the page.

Soon you are bleeding, and the bites are swelling. You begin to feel very thirsty. But drinking water barely helps.

"Either our scratches are infected, or those bugs were poisonous," Harriet says.

"This is really bad," you agree.

Harriet is the first to throw up. You join her shortly. Blood is streaming out of your bug bites, your stomach is twisting, and you feel very hot. You have a fever. You shut your eyes. You thought dinosaurs were your biggest threat here, but it turns out insects will be the death of you.

THE END

To follow another path, turn to page 11.
To learn more about the Cretaceous Period, turn to page 105.

"I'll take my chances with predators," Harriet says. "These bugs are going to eat us alive!"

"Okay, okay," you reply.

The two of you scramble out of the jungle and onto the open land. You walk through sauropod footprints bigger than sidewalk squares. You still get a few bug bites, but way fewer than before. As the sun sets behind the mountains, a beautiful orange and pink light settles over the plains.

You follow a stream until you reach a bay. Farther out, a giant sea opens up.

"I think we can spend the night here. It seems safe. Look—there's a little cave where we can stay dry and hidden."

"I think I'd feel better if we made some kind of weapon to protect ourselves first," Harriet says.

To head to the cave, turn to page 37.
To make a weapon first, turn to page 40.

You're not sure you could start a fire, so you start tearing apart the strange primitive mammals. But once you bite into the meat, your stomach turns.

"I don't think I can do it," you say, holding the meat away from your face.

"Me neither," Harriet says. "What if there's some kind of prehistoric disease in the meat?"

You toss the meat into the bushes. The bushes rustle in reaction. Something is moving in there.

"Uh, Harriet?" you say.

"I see it," she answers.

You freeze and wait. A dinosaur about the size of a large dog steps out of the bushes on its hind legs. It has a short, beaked snout and strong upper legs with fingerlike claws.

The animal hisses, and you jump back. You recognize it as a Hypsilophodon.

"Don't worry," you whisper. "It's a plant eater."

"I'm not feeling very comforted by that for some reason," she responds.

The creature looks behind you. You hear a low, raspy growl and turn around. In a nearby clearing stands another two-legged dinosaur, only this one is much bigger. It has a big, gaping jaw and sharp teeth. A tall sail of spines sticks up on its back.

"I know this one," Harriet says. "It was the answer to the second question on the test. It's an Acrocanthosaurus."

"Plant eater?" you ask hopefully.

"Nope."

Turn the page.

The Hypsilophodon is off and running. It looks like a kangaroo bounding along, and it's really fast. You can hear the Acrocanthosaurus breathing hard as it advances. It reaches the edge of the clearing and rams into a tree with its shoulder. The tree creaks and gives way. If it can get through the trees, it will get to you.

You and Harriet run. You hear the big tree crash. Then another tree crashes. The giant footsteps of the meat-eating monster get closer and closer. Harriet screams as it scoops her up. You know you're next. Your time in the Cretaceous Period has come to an end.

THE END

To follow another path, turn to page 11.
To learn more about the Cretaceous Period, turn to page 105.

"I'm not eating this thing raw," you say. "Let's see if we can make a fire."

You gather some dried leaves and bark and pile it up. You rub two sticks together for a long time. Your hands get tired, and you let Harriet take a turn. The sticks get warm. But that's the best you can do. The wood is too damp to catch fire. You don't eat the creature.

After a little searching, you find a nest of dinosaur eggs. You're not crazy about the idea of eating raw eggs, but it's not as disgusting as eating raw meat. You take an egg and crack it into your mouth. It is slimy and cool, but somehow you manage to get it down. You feel some strength seeping back into your body.

Over several days, you keep an eye on the nesting area. A community of Hypsilophodons come and go, checking their eggs.

The animals are the size of large dogs. Each one has a thick, long tail and a stout, beaked head. You know from science class that they're plant eaters.

You and Harriet start gathering wood and laying it in the sun to dry. After many attempts rubbing the dry sticks together, you finally get a few sparks. You manage to build a fire and keep it going all the time. It helps keep the bugs away.

Harriet makes a sling from vines and a stick, which she uses to fire rocks. With that, she hunts the multituberculate. You use sharp sticks and rocks to skin them and cook them over the fire.

When you gather water at the stream, you see flamingo-like pterosaurs. They are Pterodaustros, and they are peaceful and beautiful. They use long, scooped beaks to strain tiny shrimp in the shallows.

Turn the page.

Fish are coming to eat the swarms of tiny shrimp. That gives you an idea. You sharpen a spear so that you can fish.

Weeks pass, then months. You have created a tasty tea from roots and leaves you gather near your tree shelter. You eat fish, small mammals, nuts, and berries. You know the hunting patterns of the meat-eating dinosaurs, so you can easily avoid them. You tell each other stories about life back home, and sometimes you even crack jokes. It turns out you are good at living in the Early Cretaceous Period. Even though you miss home, you kind of like it here.

THE END

To follow another path, turn to page 11.
To learn more about the Cretaceous Period, turn to page 105.

"I want to get out of the open as quick as possible," you say. "It's almost dark, and we're sitting ducks."

The two of you climb down the rocks and into the entryway of the small cave. You are surprised by how easy it is to fall asleep in spite of the crazy situation. You must really be tired. Early in the morning you hear some yipping animals up above.

"Don't move," Harriet whispers.

Whatever is up there, it's better if they don't know you're here. After a while, the yipping fades away. You climb out of the cave and back up the bank.

Far across the beach near the jungle you see a pack of Deinonychuses galloping across the land. These birdlike dinosaurs are your favorite.

Turn the page.

The Deinonychuses are about 10 feet long. Their bodies and long tails are covered in feathers. Though you can't see it from here, you know that each one has deadly claws on its feet. They are beautiful creatures, but they are meat eaters. They are vicious and scary.

"I'm glad they didn't find us," Harriet says.

You look back toward the cave, where a thick mist has formed over the water. It looks familiar.

"Hey, remember Ms. Turrey's terrarium?"

Harriet looks too. "It looks just like that scene. No Triceratops, though."

That's when you remember the toy Triceratops in your hoodie pocket. You pull it out. You and Harriet climb back down the bank and into the mist. As you do, the mist begins to swirl around you.

You get dizzy and fall down, but you don't fall into water. Instead, you're lying on the hard floor of Ms. Turrey's classroom.

"Whoa, are you two okay?" someone says. It's your friend Luis.

"We're fine," you say, though you're not totally sure that's true. You certainly feel weird.

"You better get back in your seat," Luis says. "I hear Ms. Turrey coming back."

"Yes," you say as your eyes connect with Harriet's. "I guess we should finish that test."

THE END

To follow another path, turn to page 11.
To learn more about the Cretaceous Period, turn to page 105.

You agree that it's better to have something to defend yourselves. Who knows what kind of creatures are out here. You're looking for a branch to use as a club or a long stick you can sharpen into a spear. As you search, you lose sight of Harriet.

You find a stick that can be sharpened into a short spear and head back toward the cave. As you draw near, you hear the sound of animals galloping. Near the cave, dozens of Deinonychuses are running across the beach. You know about these dinosaurs. They're 10 feet long and fast. They have teeth like steak knives and strong arms and legs. And they have a long, deadly claw on each foot. Covered in feathers, they look like giant birds—if birds could tear you to shreds.

"Help!" Harriet screams.

She is running toward you, and the Deinonychuses are following. You turn to run, but it's too late. First they catch Harriet. Then they catch you. You flail your stick at them, but it's no use.

THE END

To follow another path, turn to page 11.
To learn more about the Cretaceous Period, turn to page 105.

CHAPTER 3

ALL THE BEAUTIFUL FLOWERS

You look around to find that you're in a field of flowering bushes, trees, and vines. The area is full of dazzling colors. The sun beats down on you, and immediately you begin to sweat.

You become aware of an intense buzzing. It's not just your head aching. There are millions of enormous bees, mosquitoes, and other flying, buzzing bugs you've never seen before. The insects dip and land on bright, beautiful flowers. Then they rise again and dip back, over and over. Some of them are as large as hummingbirds. The air is cloudy with them.

Turn the page.

Lying next to you are two friends from class, Harriet and Luis. There is no sign of Ms. Turrey, no sign of the terrarium from her room, and no sign of any of your other classmates. You realize Luis and Harriet must have grabbed onto you at the moment you went back in time. That's why they got pulled back with you. In the distance, a couple of looming volcanoes pipe out puffs of smoke. And across the field is a huge, duck-billed dinosaur munching happily on some plants. It has a colorful crest on top of its head.

"Whoa! What happened?" Luis says. "I hope this is part of the test!"

"Uh, I don't think it is, Luis," Harriet says. She's holding your science book open in her hands and comparing what she reads to what she sees all around. "I think we've landed in the Late Cretaceous Period."

"Amazing," you say.

You're still holding the toy Triceratops from Ms. Turrey's terrarium in your hand. You shove it into the pocket of your hoodie just as it starts to rain. It's just a sprinkle at first, but dark clouds hint at a bigger storm coming soon.

"It's sunny up on that mountain," Harriet says. "Maybe we can get up there where it's dry."

"The jungle is closer," Luis says, "and the canopy of trees will keep us dry. Kind of."

"Jungles have lots of snakes and other creatures," Harriet says.

One thing is for sure. If you wait much longer, you're going to be totally soaked.

To make a run for the mountain, turn the page.
To head for the jungle, turn to page 49.

The mountain might be far away, but the jungle sounds creepy. You start running up the incline, hoping to get out of the rain. It's not long before you stop in your tracks. That's because the duck-billed dinosaur has stopped eating and lifted its head. It stands perfectly still and looks toward the mountain.

"It's some kind of Lambeosaur," Luis says. "It's super cool, but we need to keep moving."

"Hold on," you say. That Lambeosaur is still frozen. Something is wrong. "Why isn't it moving? What does it sense?"

"You guys," Harriet says. "My book is getting wet. We might need this."

Suddenly, the Lambeosaur lets out a loud honking sound, like a deep siren. It is warning its herd that a threat is coming.

Turn the page.

When it begins running down the mountain, dozens of other Lambeosaurs come out of the surrounding hills and trees. They all run downhill.

"I think something's up there," you say.

To follow the Lambeosaurs, turn to page 51.

To keep heading up the mountain, turn to page 54.

By the time you reach the trees, you're already quite wet. But under the canopy, the rain doesn't reach you. You sit down against a tree trunk and ask Harriet if there's anything in the science book that can explain what happened to you.

"No," Harriet says, "there is definitely nothing in here about time travel."

Near your head, a flowery branch begins to twitch. You look closer. Hanging upside down beneath the leaves, a colony of flies wriggle. Each one is at least an inch long. They seem to be looking at you. You look closer. They have big, sharp jaws. Large, upside-down flying creatures with sharp teeth? Sounds a little too much like vampires to you.

"Let's get away from these things," you say.

"Those are crane flies," Harriet says.

Turn the page.

"I don't care what they are," you say. "Let's go."

The three of you start walking away, but some of the flies follow you. You wave your hands at them and start to run. Eventually you stop in a clearing to catch your breath.

That's when something grabs onto your foot. It's a massive snake.

To try to pull away, turn to page 57.
To look for a weapon, turn to page 60.

A predator is coming! Your instincts tell you to run with the Lambeosaurs. Maybe you can hide among them. Odds are whatever is coming will pick one of them instead of you.

You run after the big, duck-billed dinosaurs. They are all shrieking and honking now. Combined with their earth-shaking steps, the sound is terrifying. And those big dinosaurs are fast! You can't keep up. The plants are high, slowing you down. Soon you, Harriet, and Luis fall behind. The Lambeosaurs thunder ahead, and you are getting tired.

Breathing hard, you slow down and look over your shoulder. You shudder to see a Tyrannosaurus rex storming toward you. It's catching up very quickly, and now Luis has fallen down.

Turn the page.

Suddenly the sky ignites! A bolt of lightning strikes the field. There's an ear-shattering crack of thunder just a half second after. The flowers smolder, then go up in flames. Even in the rain, a fire begins to rage.

To keep running, turn to page 62.
To go back for Luis, turn to page 66.

"If something is chasing those Lambeosaurs, I don't want to be around when it catches them," Harriet says.

You agree. Let the Lambeosaurs be dinner, not you! They'll all be extinct soon anyway.

You run up the mountain. The flowers are mashed down in a line, making a faint path through the field, and you follow it. You realize—too late—that there can be only one reason for a path. Something walks that way a lot. You are still thinking about this when Luis grabs onto your shoulder.

"What?" you ask.

He puts his hand over your mouth and points. Up ahead is a Tyrannosaurus rex. Standing tall on its massive hind legs, it looks bigger than a house.

It opens its gigantic jaws. Its teeth look like enormous daggers ready to slice flesh. Drool streams from its mouth.

It turns one red eye on you and leans forward. Suddenly it lunges downhill toward you. Before you can think of what to do, Harriet grabs your hand and pulls you between some boulders. You crouch there, hidden in a tight space. The T. rex bangs its head against the rocks. You can smell its swampy breath. The boulders shake, but the T. rex can't get through—for now.

The giant beast lunges again at the rocks, and this time Harriet stabs at its eye with a big stick. It flinches and rears up. The T. rex roars angrily and crashes its head against the rocks again. You can feel them moving. This hiding spot won't hold for very long.

Turn the page.

You're suddenly distracted, though, as the volcano you've been climbing belches up a huge cloud of smoke. The earth rumbles, and the T. rex turns its attention to the present danger. It seems now more concerned about its own survival than eating you.

To stay hidden from the T. rex, turn to page 68.
To get away from the volcano, turn to page 71.

Your instincts take over. All you can think to do is pull, pull, pull. You try to get away.

"Help!" you yell.

Harriet finds a big rock and smashes it on the snake. You feel its muscles flinch against your leg and you pull again. You are loose for half a second, but then the snake rewraps. It gets farther up your leg. You scream again for help.

Luis is pulling its tail, trying to separate you. But the huge snake is too strong. Then it twists up around your waist. It's getting hard to breathe. Harriet hits it again and again, but it doesn't help. The snake wraps around your chest. It wraps around your neck. It opens its big mouth.

You can't breathe.

Turn the page.

Your friends are screaming. It squeezes even harder.

You can't breathe.

It hisses into your ear.

You can't—

THE END

To follow another path, turn to page 11.
To learn more about the Cretaceous Period, turn to page 105.

You fall to the ground. Near your face is a rock the size of a softball, and you grab it. Whack! The snake hisses. Just then, something scurries under the brush nearby. You feel the snake's grip relax as a brown mammal the size of a beaver steps out of the bushes. You know these from your test: multituberculates. Just as quickly as it grabbed you, the snake releases you and slithers after the mammal.

Luis says, "Thank goodness that thing looked like an easier meal than you."

You sit on the ground catching your breath. Your friends sit next to you and hug you, and you realize you've been crying. You almost died.

While you rest, Luis searches the area for water or something to eat. Harriet stays with you. For a second you think it's a bad idea to separate. But then you fall asleep.

When you wake up, it's dark. You're not sure where you are. Was the Cretaceous just a dream? You rub your eyes and look into the darkness around you. A figure is standing there. You think maybe you are home in bed.

"Mom?" you say.

The figure moves, and you realize it's not a person. It's a dinosaur about the size of an adult man. It walks on hind legs and has a hard, flat skull with spines on it. Next to you, Harriet grabs onto your arm.

"Oh no," she says.

It's a Pachycephalosaur. The spines on its skull are the last thing you see as it charges toward you.

THE END

To follow another path, turn to page 11.
To learn more about the Cretaceous Period, turn to page 105.

Luis scrambles into the tall weeds to hide.
Smoke is spreading fast, and it's hard to see.
The duck-billed dinosaurs wail their wild horn
sounds. The T. rex growls and stomps. Holding
hands so you don't get separated, you and
Harriet run through the smoke, calling for Luis
as you go. Soon the sounds of the dinosaurs fade.

Eventually you reach a lake. You're worried
about Luis, but you don't dare go back toward the
fire. Besides the flames, there's also that T. rex.
You just hope Luis has found a safe place to hide.

Through the smoke you see one of your
favorite dinosaurs: a Dracorex hogwartsia.
Named after a character from your favorite book
series, it is a plant eater with a hard, flat skull,
spiky horns, and a long muzzle. It trots away
when it sees you.

Turn the page.

When you gaze back down into the water, you see Ms. Turrey's classroom. The lake water combines with the pool of misty water inside the terrarium.

"I think this must be the portal home," Harriet says.

Overjoyed, you reach into your hoodie and pull out the toy Triceratops. You take Harriet's hand again and step into the lake.

"Wait!" Harriet says. Right as she speaks, you feel the world spin.

When you open your eyes again, you're in the classroom. Your friends are looking at you in amazement. You're home! But your happiness quickly fades when you see Harriet's troubled face.

"I said, 'Wait!'"

"Why?" you say.

But then you realize why. You left Luis behind. A sick feeling comes over you. How will you live with the knowledge that you abandoned him?

THE END

To follow another path, turn to page 11.
To learn more about the Cretaceous Period, turn to page 105.

"We have to help Luis!" you say.

The two of you run up the mountain toward the T. rex. The fire spreads quickly. The flames rage dangerously close. All sorts of creatures are dashing past you—mammals, lizards, and snakes. Birds are flying away from the mountain. The insects have disappeared.

"Luis!" Harriet screams.

"Luis!" you scream.

There's no answer. You keep searching. Dinosaurs run past you. Some are the size of big dogs. Some are the size of people. Some are much bigger. You dodge the great legs of the T. rex. Maybe it's not even the same one. Four-legged dinosaurs also run past. All the creatures are terrified, running for their lives. Flames rise into the sky.

The smoke makes it hard to breathe and to see. Something knocks you to the ground. Pain races up your arm into your shoulder. Your hand dangles like something dead—your wrist is broken. But you have worse problems. Something large steps on your leg and crushes the bones. You can't get up. You can't see. You don't know where your friends are.

You curl up and cover your head. You hope Luis and Harriet will survive, even though you will not.

THE END

To follow another path, turn to page 11.
To learn more about the Cretaceous Period, turn to page 105.

Is the volcano erupting? You're not sure. But you are sure that there is a T. rex out there somewhere. You tell Luis and Harriet that it feels safer here, where at least you won't be eaten.

"Good point," Luis says.

You hunch behind the rocks and wait. You keep watch from your cove, but you do not see the T. rex anymore.

It was already hot, but now it's getting much hotter. All three of you are sweating. Something is crackling. You look out from the rocks and see lava streaming down the mountain. Trees and bushes and all those flowering plants are going up in flames.

"Um, you guys?" you say. "I think we better get out of here."

"I think you're right," Harriet says.

Turn the page.

You jump out of the rocks and start running downhill as fast as you can. Looking behind you, you see a fresh lava stream lapping at the earth. You trip over a big tree root and get the wind knocked out of you. Luis turns and lifts you up. The air is scorching hot. You run to catch up to Harriet. But the lava is coming too fast. You were worried about making it home, but you won't even make it to the bottom of this mountain.

THE END

To follow another path, turn to page 11.
To learn more about the Cretaceous Period, turn to page 105.

"I think this volcano is erupting," Harriet says nervously.

"We better get out of here!" Luis cries.

"What about that T. rex?" you ask.

"She's smart," Harriet replies. "She's running away from the volcano!"

You climb out of the rocky hideout and run down the mountain. Fat streams of lava seem to chase you. The sky is darkening as the volcano belches black smoke. The flowery field catches fire. Nearly out of breath, you get off the mountain just in time.

You run until you reach a lake with a wide, muddy beach. Walking along the shore, you find a cave that seems safe from the fire. The three of you climb inside and wait. You drink some fresh water from a stream that trickles down the wall.

Turn the page.

A few days later, the fire dies down. You climb out of the cave and look around. The landscape is smoking and barren.

You walk all day looking for food. You find some nuts and a tree with yellow fruits on it. You're so hungry that everything tastes amazing.

Days pass. Then weeks. You and your friends make a home in the cave by the lake. You collect nuts and fruits, and soon you have a large store of food.

"Do you think Ms. Turrey knows where we are?" you ask one day.

"I hope so," Luis says. "Maybe she'll get us home."

In the meantime, you have gotten very good at surviving in the Cretaceous Period. You know you can wait a long time, if you have to.

THE END

To follow another path, turn to page 11.
To learn more about the Cretaceous Period, turn to page 105.

CHAPTER 4

SEAFOOD SPECIAL

You stand up in the mud and take a step forward. But there is nowhere for your foot to land. You fall off a cliff and splash into frigid water. The mist thickens around you. You shiver.

"Hello?" you call.

"Over here!" someone says.

"Luis? Is that you?"

"It's me!" he says.

You swim toward the voice. Finally, you find him. His lips are trembling and turning blue. It sure is cold!

"We have to get out of this water!" you say. "I fell off a cliff around here somewhere."

Turn the page.

"Let's swim this way," Luis says.

You follow him through the mist, which is quickly turning into rain. A strip of land appears out of the gloom, and you crawl up onto the beach. You're both lying in the mud catching your breath.

"You okay?" you ask.

"I'm okay," Luis says. "You?"

"I'm good."

You get up and walk up the beach toward a rocky outcropping you can barely see through the mist. You find a place to hide under the rocks until the rain stops. When it does, the sun comes out, and the temperature spikes. You start sweating. You step out of the rocks into the blazing sun. Your clothes dry out quickly. You're so hot you almost wish they'd stayed wet.

You look around. You're on a small rocky island. About 50 yards across the lagoon is a larger landmass where you can see fruit trees. You peer into the water and see a school of giant rays, even bigger than manta rays, swimming past.

To swim for the large landmass, turn the page.
To explore your island, turn to page 81.

You and Luis decide to swim for the shore. The rays swim beneath you. You look into the water and watch them glide right below you. They're as big as cars! Luckily, they don't seem to mind you swimming with them.

When you reach the beach, you and Luis scramble up out of the water as fast as you can. You lay in the sun drying off for a few minutes.

You're about to go check out the fruit on the nearby trees when you hear a loud squawk. In the trees at the top of the beach, a dinosaur stares at you. It reminds you of an ostrich. It has a long, sharp beak and feathers all over. Its arms and legs have long claws. You freeze. You think this is a Troodon. You remember studying them in school. Troodons likely ate both plants and animals. Though they probably hunted small animals, you still don't like the way it's looking at you.

Turn the page.

The Troodon raises its wings to scare you. It works. As you back away toward the water, you bump into Luis.

"Better stop," he says.

You turn around. He's staring at a 10-foot crocodile at the edge of the water. It opens its big jaws and claps them shut.

To go toward the Troodon, turn to page 84.
To go toward the crocodile, turn to page 86.

"Let's not get back in that water," you say, pointing to the giant rays. "I feel safer here."

"I agree," Luis says.

You scout the island looking for fresh water and shelter. You walk through a swampy stand of trees and come out at a cliff edge. This must be where you fell off when you first arrived. Birds and several pteranodons soar overhead. Out over the water, you hear splashes and churning waves.

What is creating this ruckus? A giant head rises out of the water on a long, powerful neck. A sauropod wades through the water and begins chomping on some trees nearby.

The sauropod has a beardlike frill on its throat. You recognize it as an Alamosaurus. Compared to it, you feel like an ant.

Turn the page.

Luis gasps, and the massive creature startles. It looks at you for a second, then lifts its tail out of the water. It's like a massive oak trunk, except it flexes like a whip.

The tail thrashes into the water and a giant wave pounds up onto the island and knocks you down. You get up, and the tail swings again. This time it's coming right at you. Luis jumps into the water. You're not sure if that's a good idea, but then neither is staying here.

To join Luis in the water, turn to page 88.
To hide behind the trees for protection, turn to page 90.

No way are you going to let some prehistoric crocodile take a shot at you. You run up the beach toward the Troodon. It opens its wings again and squawks. You know that croc is lumbering after you, so you keep charging ahead. The Troodon turns and runs off along the sand.

You look back. The crocodile chased you halfway up the beach, but now it sits and looks at you. It's a fast sprinter, but those short legs make it hard to run that quickly for a long time. It just snaps its jaws at you a couple times, then turns to waddle back to the water. All the muscles in your body relax when you realize you're safe—for now. Your heart is still pounding as you turn your attention to the trees.

"Look at these enormous fruits," you say.

Luis joins you at the tree and you shake a branch until a couple of orange fruits fall down. They're as big as coconuts with a soft, fleshy peel. You poke your thumb into the top of one and rip it open. It tastes like honey and orange.

"Amazing!" Luis says.

You each eat one of the fruits. Then you have another. You are relaxing in the sand with full bellies when you hear something rustling in the bushes. It's coming from deep in the jungle. It sounds slow. And it sounds big. The sun is getting low in the sky, meaning night is coming soon. A fire could keep you warm and scare away predators. On the other hand, you might want to find out just what's out there.

To try to build a fire on the beach, turn to page 92.
To investigate, turn to page 94.

You know the Troodon is not likely to hunt you. Even if there's a pack of them, you are too big. But somehow it seems too scary to get any closer. At least a crocodile is something you've seen before.

So you linger on the beach. Luis keeps an eye on the croc, and you watch the Troodon.

"He's coming closer," Luis warns.

"More Troodons are coming out of the woods," you say.

"He's coming closer," Luis says again.

You turn to look. The croc is stepping slowly and surely toward you. You look back to the Troodons. Suddenly, they all squawk and run away.

"Let's go!" Luis says as he runs past you.

You start running, but the croc latches onto your foot. You try to twist away, but its jaws are too powerful. Your leg is crushed. The croc is pulling you backward toward the water.

"Luis!" you yell.

Your fingers rake lines in the sand, trying to hold your ground. Luis comes and kicks the crocodile in the belly, but it doesn't do any good. In a few seconds, it has pulled you under the water.

THE END

To follow another path, turn to page 11.
To learn more about the Cretaceous Period, turn to page 105.

It's best to stick together, even if this is crazy! You jump off the cliff and plunge back into the cold water. You stay underwater and swim in the opposite direction of the Alamosaurus. Even underwater, you hear its giant tail hitting the island. When you finally surface, you look up. The place where you were standing is rubble.

"Luis!" you call out. "Luis, where are you?"

Finally, you see Luis swimming toward the mainland. You swim after him. Suddenly a fish almost as long as a minivan swims upward toward you. It has gaping, sharp-looking buck teeth. It's a Xiphactinus, and it opens its mouth to chomp you. It looks like your time in the Cretaceous Period is over. You only hope Luis finds a way to survive.

THE END

To follow another path, turn to page 11.
To learn more about the Cretaceous Period, turn to page 105.

You turn and run toward the other side of the island. The tail crashes onto the cliff and smashes trees and rocks, which crumble into the sea. It is an awesome sight. You push through the thick branches and leaves. Once you arrive at the other side of the island, you climb down to the beach where you and Luis first came up. He is there in the mud waiting for you.

"Let's get off this island," you say. "And away from that big guy."

"Good call," Luis says.

You begin to swim back across the lagoon. Your limbs are tired, and your heart is racing furiously. You still haven't caught your breath, and you're afraid you won't make it to the island in the distance. Luis looks pretty tired too.

You're both beginning to flounder when a giant sea turtle surfaces nearby. It's bigger than a van.

"I don't know if I can swim much more," Luis gasps. "Maybe we should get a ride on that guy."

"He seems pretty relaxed," you reply. "It might be our best shot.

Luis climbs onto its back, and you join him. You both lean up and grab onto the collar of its shell.

The turtle drags you to the mainland, without even seeming to notice you're there. As you get close to land, you slip off into the water and wade ashore.

"I'm tired of being wet and cold," Luis says.

"Me too," you agree. "Let's build a fire."

Turn the page.

You quickly gather dried twigs, leaves, and grass, while Luis clears out a shallow hole. Luis takes off his watch and breaks the glass off the face. He holds it so it captures the sun's rays and concentrates them on the pile of kindling. It's not long before the grass and leaves begin to smoke, and Luis blows on them gently. Soon, you have bright flames.

You gather bigger twigs and dry sun-bleached driftwood. Before long, evening is upon you, and your fire is raging.

Suddenly, you hear a series of loud cracks coming from the forest. A large tree tumbles over and lands in the sand near your fire. An Ankylosaurus comes out of the woods after it. The tank-shaped dinosaur stops to munch on the leaves of the tree, which are now conveniently at ground level.

It looks at you. Its tail looks like a stone beach ball attached to the end of a whip. You gulp nervously as it swishes that club of a tail around like a happy house cat. To your relief, it eats all the leaves and moves on.

After it's gone, you're still not alone. More monsters lurk in the woods. You hear them snorting, pushing through the leaves, and occasionally growling or yelping at one another. Maybe you should find something to defend yourself with, but you don't really want to leave the comforting glow of the fire.

To spend the night by your fire, turn to page 96.
To look for a weapon, turn to page 100.

You don't want any surprises in the middle of the night. You slip into the trees for a look around. You follow the noises—chomping, snorting, and snuffling. A tree cracks and falls. You hear a deep, rasping cough, and then out of the darkness shuffles an Ankylosaurus. For a moment, you and Luis are in a staring contest with the massive turtlelike dinosaur. Then you see something change in its eyes. Fear. It's never seen a human before. You almost laugh at the thought of this monstrous beast being afraid of you.

It turns—much quicker than you would think such a big animal could do—and suddenly its big tail is whizzing through the air. The end of the tail is a giant, hard ball with spikes. It crushes you and Luis in a single blow.

THE END

To follow another path, turn to page 11.
To learn more about the Cretaceous Period, turn to page 105.

You and Luis take turns collecting wood nearby and stoking the fire all through the night. In the morning, you wake up on the beach under the baking sun.

You're barely awake when you hear a deep snort behind you. You turn and see a Triceratops walking across the beach. From up on a berm, an Albertosaurus climbs down toward you as well. This quick theropod is a lot like a T. rex, but smaller. It has its eyes on the Triceratops.

The Triceratops does not intend to become anyone's dinner today. It lowers its head and charges, goring its enemy with one of its long, spear-like tusks. The Albertosaurus screams, and the sand around it darkens with blood.

The Triceratops turns and looks at you. You should probably be scared, but for some reason, you're not. You recall the toy Triceratops in Ms. Turrey's terrarium.

"Hi," you say.

"Are you kidding me?" Luis asks. "Talking to a dinosaur? He just gored that other guy."

"I think it wants us to follow it," you say.

You grab Luis's arm and pull him after the Triceratops. He follows along reluctantly. The beast leads you down the beach to a rocky pool at the edge of the lagoon. A mist hovers over the water. It looks like the terrarium. You step past the Triceratops. You can't explain it, but you trust the dinosaur.

Turn the page.

Dragging Luis, you step into the misty pool. The air begins to swirl. Then a powerful wind kicks in. When it settles, you are standing in the classroom next to the terrarium.

"Students, please sit down," Ms. Turrey says.

"What?" you say, still trying to take in the sudden shift in surroundings.

"I'm glad you like my diorama," she says, "but you do have a test to finish."

With a sigh of relief, you go back to your desk. You've never been so happy to take a test in your life.

THE END

To follow another path, turn to page 11.
To learn more about the Cretaceous Period, turn to page 105.

There's no way you'll be able to sleep here anyway, so you walk along the beach looking for something to throw or swing at a predator. You also gather wood to burn.

Somehow you survive the night. Over the next several days you collect rocks to throw, fruits and roots to eat, and wood for the fire. You and Luis take turns eating and foraging. It is a boring life, but you are alive. That is all you care about for now.

Then one day you are lying on the beach looking at the sky when you see a raging ball of fire plummet from space. It screams and crackles louder than anything you've ever heard. The sky turns an amazing purple and yellow as the asteroid crashes into Earth far, south of you.

Turn the page.

"That's the asteroid," Luis says. His face is streaked with mud. His eyes and skin are red from sunburn. His shirt is torn and bloody. "The one that hits Chicxulub."

"The one that killed the dinosaurs?" you say.

"That's the one."

Over the next few hours, you watch as the sky to the south grows dark with smoke and ash. You know that massive waves will make their way across miles and miles of ocean, crash onto land, and flood it. You can't see much of the destruction yet, but you know it is coming. You can smell the smoke. Fires are coming.

"We're going to die here," you say. "We're going to die in the Cretaceous Period."

"I'm afraid you're right," Luis says.

He doesn't look scared or worried. You've been barely surviving for so many weeks by now. You've fought off dinosaurs and other prehistoric animals. You've wondered if you'd ever see your families again. Maybe a quick death is the best you can hope for.

THE END

To follow another path, turn to page 11.
To learn more about the Cretaceous Period, turn to page 105.

CHAPTER 5

THE CRETACEOUS PERIOD

The Cretaceous Period was dominated by dinosaurs and ended with their extinction. It started about 145 million years ago, following the Jurassic Period, and lasted about 79 million years. During this time, Earth was reshaping itself as the supercontinent Pangaea drifted apart. By the end of the period, oceans had filled in the gaps between continents, which looked a lot like they do now. Temperatures all over the globe were warmer than they are now.

One of the most important features of the Cretaceous Period was the development of flowering plants. They spread across the land, and flying insects such as bees and wasps pollinated them. Other insects, such as butterflies, ants, beetles, and grasshoppers, also spread.

Ancestors of many modern bird types appeared during this period, including cormorants, pelicans, and sandpipers. Mammals, especially multituberculates, lived comfortably in the forests. Frogs, salamanders, snakes, turtles, and crocodiles, thrived. Sharks and rays swam through the oceans alongside enormous plesiosaurs and mosasaurs.

But the stars of the Cretaceous Period were the dinosaurs. Gigantic sauropods lumbered across the land in herds. Birdlike dinosaurs lived in great numbers over most of the globe. Massive horned dinosaurs such as Triceratops lumbered on land. Terrifying meat eaters such as Spinosaurus and Tyrannosaurus rex sat at the top of the food chain.

About 65 million years ago, an asteroid or comet about the size of a small city streaked out of the sky. It struck the Yucatan Peninsula of Mexico.

The explosion it caused was 2 million times stronger than the most powerful human-made bomb. Debris from the explosion flew into the atmosphere and landed, still burning, causing fires across the globe. Earthquakes, volcanic eruptions, and monstrous waves called tsunamis rippled out from the crash site. The smoke and debris in the air blocked out sunlight for years, starving plants of the energy they needed. Plants died, and the Earth grew very cold.

The crater left behind by the explosion has been called the Chicxulub crater after the town that now lies near its center. Scientists are not certain if the Chicxulub collision was the only event that caused more than half of the planet's species to go extinct. It may have been one in a series of collisions that, along with the eruption of many volcanoes, brought an end to the Cretaceous Period.

TIMELINE

252 million years ago •••

Paleozoic Era
time of ancient life

Mesozoic Era
time of dinosaurs

251 ••••••••••• 200
million years ago   million years ago

TRIASSIC PERIOD

200 •••••••••••••••••• 146
million years ago   million years ago

JURASSIC PERIOD

180 MILLION YEARS AGO
The Atlantic Ocean and Indian Ocean form as the supercontinent Pangaea breaks apart.

252 MILLION YEARS AGO
A mass extinction marks the end of the Paleozoic Era, sparking a rapid change in animal and plant life. The Mesozoic Era begins, with the first of its three periods, the Triassic. The age of reptiles begins.

210-200 MILLION YEARS AGO
Triassic Period ends, and Jurassic begins.

190 MILLION YEARS AGO
The first mammals appear on Earth.

230-220 MILLION YEARS AGO
The first dinosaurs appear.

145 MILLION YEARS AGO
Jurassic Period ends, and Cretaceous begins.

··•65 million years ago

Cenozoic Era
time of mammals

145•··•65
million years ago   million years ago

CRETACEOUS PERIOD

100-66 MILLION YEARS AGO
Late Cretaceous
T. rex reigns.

65 MILLION YEARS AGO
Chicxulub Asteroid impacts Mexico. Dinosaurs go extinct. Cretaceous Period ends. Cenozoic Era begins with the Paleogene Period. Earth recovers, temperatures warm, and modern mammals appear.

146-100 MILLION YEARS AGO
Early Cretaceous
First flowering plants evolve, such as magnolia and ficus. Some groups of modern insects appear, including bees, wasps, beetles, and ants.

23 MILLION YEARS AGO
Neogene Period of the Cenezoic Era begins. Grass spreads. New species of mammals and other animals evolve.

COULD YOU SURVIVE
THE JURASSIC PERIOD?

BY MATT DOEDEN

ILLUSTRATED BY JUAN CALLE

TABLE OF CONTENTS

INTRODUCTION

YOU are an ordinary kid going about your everyday life. Suddenly you find yourself in a strange place and a strange time. It's a period from long ago. The world looks different than anything you've ever seen before. Terrifying beasts roam the land. Danger lurks at every turn. Where will you find shelter? How will you get food? Will you ever see your friends and family again? Most importantly of all, can you survive?

Chapter One sets the scene. Then you choose which path to take. Follow the directions at the bottom of each page. The choices you make determine what happens next. After you finish your path, go back and read the others for more adventures.

YOU CHOOSE the path you take through the Jurassic Period!

Turn the page to begin your adventure.

CHAPTER 1

LOST IN TIME

"Look at that!" gasps your friend Eduardo.

He's pointing toward a huge Stegosaurus fossil on display at the science museum.

"Can you imagine running into one of those? Man, I wish I could see one in real life!"

"Boring," says Jasmine. "Where's the T. rex? I want to see a *real* dinosaur!"

Eduardo's face turns red. When it comes to dinosaurs, he's a fanatic. He fights the urge to snap at Jasmine as he grips the thick *Guide to the Jurassic* he bought at the gift shop.

"Jasmine," he says. "The sign says 'Jurassic Period.' Tyrannosaurus rex didn't live during the Jurassic, no matter what the movies say."

Turn the page.

"Hey," you say, glancing over your shoulder. "Our class is headed toward the Ancient Egypt exhibit. We should . . ."

Eduardo cuts you off. "Just a second. Check this out!"

The three of you step up to the base of the Stegosaurus skeleton. "Put your hand on it."

"I don't think we're supposed to touch it," Jasmine warns.

"Nobody's looking," Eduardo responds. "Imagine what the world must have been like."

All three of you touch the fossil. It's smooth and cool to the touch. You imagine what this animal would have looked like when it was alive.

Suddenly a wave of dizziness sweeps over you. Your stomach churns. You feel like you're falling. Then everything goes black.

When you regain consciousness, something is wrong. The museum is gone. You're outside, lying in a sunbaked clearing. Tall trees and strange ferns grow all around you. The air smells damp.

Eduardo wakes up next to you, his book still clutched under his arm. And there's Jasmine, just starting to sit up and rub her eyes.

"What . . . where?" Eduardo stammers.

None of this makes any sense. You look up. The sky is brilliant blue, dotted with clouds.

A shadow passes overhead. Is it a bird? It's huge! You squint your eyes and scream. A creature soars high above—a creature that should not be there.

"It's . . . it's . . . a pterosaur!" Eduardo gasps.

"This can't be possible," Jasmine says. "It can't be real!"

Turn the page.

Far in the distance, you hear a low roaring sound. Some sort of animal made it. And from the sound of it, it's a *huge* animal. That, combined with the strange plant life and the pterosaur in the sky, leaves no doubt of what has happened, no matter how insane it sounds.

"Umm, Eduardo," you whisper. "I don't think we have to imagine the Jurassic anymore. I'm afraid we're in it."

You stand at the edge of a dense forest, which lies to your north. The land east and south drops off into what looks like a large wetland area. An open prairie covered with ferns lies to the west.

"Where do we go?" Eduardo asks.

"You're the dinosaur expert," Jasmine snaps. "Why don't you tell us?"

Both of them look at you. Someone has to make a decision.

To head into the forest, turn to page 121.

To venture out onto the prairie, turn to page 157.

To wade into the wetlands, turn to page 187.

CHAPTER 2

THE PREHISTORIC FOREST

As another bone-chilling roar rolls over the land, you suddenly feel very exposed.

"Let's take cover in the forest!" you shout.

The three of you rush toward the thick trees and bushes. Huge ferns slap at your face as you charge into the brush. The branches of large pine trees hang low, forcing you to duck and weave as you run. Jasmine stumbles over a tree root but pops right back up to her feet. The farther in you go, the thicker the brush gets. Small flies swarm all over.

Your heart races when Eduardo suddenly screams. Is it a dinosaur?

Turn the page.

"It's huge! Get it away! Get it away!" he shouts, swatting at the air.

Then you see it. An enormous bug that looks like a dragonfly buzzes around his face.

"Wow, it's as long as my arm!" Jasmine gasps.

You've never seen anything like it. Eduardo keeps shouting, trying to swat the insect away. It finally buzzes away deeper into the forest.

"Aw, Ed, be nice. He's just welcoming us to the Jurassic," Jasmine says with a nervous laugh.

You start giggling, too. Then she laughs some more. Which makes you laugh even harder. Eduardo just scowls.

"If you two are ready to stop being ridiculous," Eduardo says, "I'd remind you that we're trapped in the past and surrounded by creatures that probably want to eat us."

Of course, he's right. It's so absurd that laughing is almost all you can do.

"OK," you say, calming yourself. "Let's think. We'll need food."

"And shelter," Eduardo suggests.

"I'm thirsty," Jasmine says. "We're going to need water before anything else."

To search for shelter, turn the page.
To look for food and water, turn to page 127.

"We need to find somewhere safe," you decide. "Let's look for shelter."

Ahead, the land rises into rolling hills. Eduardo suggests that maybe you can find a cave or a narrow canyon in that direction. Getting there won't be easy, though. The forest is dense. You scramble through thick brush and trees for what seems like an hour. When you finally find a large clearing, it's filled with the most amazing creatures you've ever seen. You hang back in the trees, staring.

"Brachiosaurus!" Eduardo says. "Look at them! They make an elephant look tiny."

The huge beasts lumber through the clearing, munching on trees. They're fantastic. And luckily, they don't pay you any attention. The only bad thing about them is the smell. It reminds you of a cattle barn.

Turn the page.

"This isn't a safari," Jasmine says. "We can't just stop and take in the sights. Let's give them plenty of room and keep going."

"Are you kidding?" Eduardo says. "We're the only humans to have ever seen these animals in real life! We have to get a closer look. And take some pictures!"

To keep going and move around the Brachiosauruses, turn to page 140.

To get a closer look at the Brachiosauruses, turn to page 150.

Jasmine is right. All that running has left you feeling thirsty, and your stomach is already beginning to rumble.

"We can't do anything if we're dying of thirst and hunger," you decide. "This is a forest. It should be loaded with things we can eat."

The three of you move across the forest floor, scanning for food.

"Where are all the flowers?" Jasmine asks. "Shouldn't they be blooming everywhere?"

"There were no flowers in the Jurassic," Eduardo says. "They hadn't evolved yet."

"I guess that means no gigantic bees to worry about then," Jasmine says. "That's good news."

"But no flowers means no fruit," you point out. "That makes our food search more difficult."

Turn the page.

"Look at that," Jasmine says, pointing to the ground. "Animal tracks!"

Sure enough, a set of small tracks leads toward a stand of pine trees. If there's no fruit, maybe you can find some meat to eat.

"Hold on," Eduardo says. "I hear the sound of running water. There could be a stream."

To follow the animal tracks, go to the next page.
To look for the source of the running water, turn to page 130.

"Maybe it's something we can eat," you say, looking at the tracks.

Reluctantly, Eduardo agrees to follow the tracks with you and Jasmine. You follow them along a muddy stretch of forest floor, right up to a small tree.

"Look," Jasmine says, pointing at a branch.

There, munching on a seed, sits a furry little . . . something. It's about the size of a squirrel, but longer and leaner. It looks at you with brown eyes, curious, but not afraid. It's a mammal.

Jasmine reaches for a large rock. She raises the rock over her head as she slowly approaches the small animal.

"Here goes nothing," she says. "Sorry little fella', but we need food."

To tell Jasmine to stop, turn to page 132.
To continue the hunt, turn to page 142.

"A stream? That means water!" you say.

The three of you tromp through the forest to a small stream. The water rushes toward a larger river beyond. On the far bank, you see several large Ceratosauruses, but they don't notice you.

"Eduardo, were there fish in the Jurassic Period?" you ask.

"Of course," he says. "Fish evolved long before land creatures. This river might be full of them."

You smile. "Well then, I think we've just found our source of both food *and* water."

"We should make camp here," Jasmine says.

Eduardo nods. "Maybe. It would keep us close to food and water. Of course, other animals would want to stay close too. That could be a problem."

To suggest a different spot to make camp, turn to page 135.

To set up a camp near the river, turn to page 151.

"Jasmine, don't do it!" you cry.

At the sound of your voice, the little mammal scurries away up the tree.

"What was that?" Jasmine asks with a scowl.

"Think about it," you say. "We're mammals. What if that was an ancient ancestor?"

"Don't be ridiculous," Jasmine snaps at you, tossing the rock aside. "Now we're all going to go hungry."

"I don't think so," Eduardo interrupts. He's munching on a handful of seeds. "Look, these are what that little animal was eating. They're not bad!"

He's right. The seeds aren't bad, and they're everywhere. The three of you eat your fill, feeling stronger by the moment.

Then you hear a rustling sound from behind you. Slowly, you turn around. A dinosaur emerges into the clearing, about a football field's distance from where you stand. The animal is as long as a pickup truck and walks on two legs. Its razor-sharp teeth gleam in the sunlight that trickles through to the forest floor.

"Ceratosaurus," Eduardo whispers. "Predator."

The dinosaur hasn't seen you yet. It's sniffing at the air, possibly confused by your unfamiliar scent. You suddenly feel like the small mammal Jasmine was about to kill.

To remain still and silent, turn the page.
To run, turn to page 143.

"Don't move," you whisper.

You watch the huge beast out of the corner of your eye. The dinosaur takes a few steps in your direction. Its head moves slowly back and forth as it sniffs the air. Your heart races.

It's going to see us! you think. Your hands are shaking. Your knees are about to buckle. You're doomed!

Just when you can't take it anymore, something rushes out of the brush. It's a small reptile. The Ceratosaurus springs into action, chasing the reptile into the forest.

"Phew!" Jasmine gasps. All three of you collapse to the forest floor.

"We're never going to be safe here, are we?" Eduardo asks.

Turn to page 141.

"I don't think that's a good idea," you argue, pointing at the Ceratosaurus on the far bank. "All kinds of animals use this river as a source of food and water. If we stay here, we'll just be another item on the menu for predators."

"Hmm, good point," Eduardo says. "Let's collect some water and look somewhere else for a place to camp."

Luckily, Jasmine has a large, stainless-steel water bottle. You'll need to boil the water to make it safe to drink, but it's a perfect opportunity to fill it. You could fill it in this small trickle of water and stay hidden, or you could risk going to the river to fill it faster.

To fill it from the small stream, turn the page.
To go to the bank of the large river to fill it, turn to page 148.

"Let's stay away from the main river for now," you suggest. "There's no way of knowing what might be lurking there."

Jasmine slowly fills the bottle in the small stream, and you make your way deeper into the forest. As you move along the forest floor, you can't help but feel like it's only a matter of time before some Jurassic beast spots you and decides to see how you taste. Meanwhile, Jasmine collects cones from the forest's dense pine trees.

"Pine nuts," she says. "We can eat these!"

The nuts don't taste very good, and they're a lot of work to get, but at least it's something. It gives you confidence you'll find more things to eat as you explore. You move along a rocky ridge. In the distance, you spot several openings.

"Look, caves," you say. "They're perfect!"

"Umm, there's a small problem," Jasmine interrupts. "Actually a huge problem!"

Between you and the caves stands the biggest dinosaur you've seen yet. It has a body the size of a bulldozer, a broad tail, and a long neck. Instinctively, you start to back up.

"Wait," Eduardo says. "It's eating plants. I think it's some sort of sauropod. If we give it some space, it's not going to care about us."

You look back at the beast. If Eduardo is wrong, you'll all be dinosaur food.

To move around the sauropod to the cave, turn the page.
To turn around, turn to page 147.

It will be dark soon, and you don't want to be trapped out here when the sun sets.

"OK, slowly then," you say.

The three of you carefully sneak across the clearing. The sauropod munches away on a tree, paying no attention to you at all. The three of you rush into the cave, falling to the floor with relief.

It's a small cave, but the narrow opening will protect you from larger predators. There are signs that some other animal once made its home here, but luckily the cave appears to be abandoned now. You have the uneasy feeling that this little cave might be home now.

Turn to page 141.

As much as you would love to watch the giant beasts, you need to find shelter before sundown. You give the enormous dinosaurs plenty of room as you move around them. Once you reach the tree-covered hills, you find exactly what you're looking for—some small caves.

"They're perfect," Jasmine says. "No predators are going to get us here."

You're exhausted. You collapse in one of the caves and fall asleep. When you wake, you're sure it was all a dream. But no. You're still here, lying in a dusty cave, 150 million years in the past.

Go to the next page.

Every day is a struggle for survival. Over time, you and your friends find sources of food and water. A small cave provides the perfect shelter from the Ceratosaurus, Torvosaurus, and other predators that roam the forest floor. You learn the patterns and movements of the dinosaurs and other Jurassic creatures. Slowly, you build a life in this strange time.

Years pass. As you grow into adulthood, you become restless. You dream of exploring more of the world. But the thought of leaving the only other human beings on the planet is terrifying.

You suggest striking out and leaving the forest. But Eduardo and Jasmine are determined to remain here, where they know they're somewhat safe.

To leave Eduardo and Jasmine to see the world, turn to page 144.

To remain safely in the hills, turn to page 154.

You hold your breath as Jasmine slams the rock with pinpoint accuracy. The animal never even tries to get away. But the moment it falls to the ground, you feel queasy. Your head spins. Beside you, Eduardo collapses to the ground. You and Jasmine both fall to your knees, grasping at your heads.

As you watch your friends, they seem to be fading away. It's almost like you can see right through them.

"Oh no," Eduardo says. "What have we done!"

"What?" gasps Jasmine. She's fading away.

"A mammal," Eduardo whispers. "You just killed one of our ancestors."

Your last thought as you fade away is that you may have just doomed the entire human race.

THE END

To follow another path, turn to page 119.
To learn more about the Jurassic Period, turn to page 211.

Your heart races. The Ceratosaurus sniffs again at the air. You can hear its huge claws scraping against rock.

As quickly as you can, you spring to your feet and start to sprint toward a thick stand of trees. The great predator screeches as it targets you. It's blindingly fast. You never even stood a chance. It knocks you to the ground with a sickening thud. The powerful impact knocks you out instantly. That's a good thing, because what comes next is much, much worse.

THE END

To follow another path, turn to page 119.
To learn more about the Jurassic Period, turn to page 211.

"I'm sorry," you tell your friends. "I just can't stay here anymore. I need to see what's out there. I really wish you would join me."

Eduardo just shakes his head. Jasmine frowns. With a hug for each, you say goodbye.

"I'll come back one day," you promise.

With that, you strike out on the adventure of a lifetime. You see a great Brontosaurus grazing. You walk with herds of Stegosauruses. You narrowly escape being eaten by a fierce Allosaurus, twice! You even gain a companion—a young Dryosaurus that seems to think you're its mother.

It's an experience unlike any other. Yet in the dark of night, you're lonely. During the days, you often find yourself gazing out to the horizon, wondering if your friends are still out there.

Turn the page.

Years later, you go back home. Your friends welcome you back with open arms and a surprise. Their little family of two has grown. They have a daughter, Kiara! It's a new life in an old time. But for the first time, this place and time finally feel like home.

THE END

To follow another path, turn to page 119.
To learn more about the Jurassic Period, turn to page 211.

"That dinosaur could crush a car," you say. "We can't risk it. Let's find some other shelter."

Eduardo shrugs and follows you. You walk for hours without finding shelter. The sun sets, and darkness falls over the forest.

"This is bad," Jasmine says.

The three of you nestle together against a large rock. Every snap and crunch on the forest floor makes your heart race. Then you hear a different sort of sound. It's a huffing sound . . . breathing. You scan for the source of it, but you can't see anything.

When the beast makes its charge, you have no chance. It's so dark you never even see what kind of dinosaur it is. The only good news is that the attack doesn't last long. Neither did your trip to the Jurassic.

THE END

To follow another path, turn to page 119.
To learn more about the Jurassic Period, turn to page 211.

"This stream is so shallow, it will be hard to fill the bottle," you say. "Let's try the river."

You navigate over rocks and mud to reach the river's bank. The water is a bit brown from sediment. Everything smells damp.

Jasmine hands you the bottle. You lower it into the river, letting the water flow inside.

"It's so peaceful here," you say. "I think this is going to be the perfect spot for—"

It all happens in an instant. An enormous shape bursts forth from the water. All you can see are jaws and teeth. You have just enough time to realize what it is—a giant crocodile—before it grabs you and drags you under the muddy water. Hopefully, Eduardo and Jasmine learn from your mistake.

THE END

To follow another path, turn to page 119.
To learn more about the Jurassic Period, turn to page 211.

"Come on!" Jasmine says, moving toward the grazing herd. She points to the phone you're carrying. "Take my picture with a dinosaur!"

You laugh. Jasmine carefully moves close to one of the huge beasts. She doesn't even come up to its knee. With a chuckle, you raise your phone.

"No wait!" Eduardo shouts—but not in time.

You press the button, and the camera clicks. The flash startles the Brachiosaurus. It raises up on its hind legs, then crashes back down to the ground. All of the giant dinosaurs begin to run.

It's a stampede! The huge dinosaurs crush everything in their path. You try to dart in between their legs but fail. A giant foot comes down, and the world goes black.

THE END

To follow another path, turn to page 119.
To learn more about the Jurassic Period, turn to page 211.

"There might not be any place in this world that's safe for us," you say. "This will have to do for now."

The three of you get to work building a camp. You use fallen branches to construct a small lean-to shelter. Over the next week, you master fishing. Eduardo manages to trap some small mammals and reptiles. You go into the forest collecting seeds and nuts. You hear large creatures in the forest several times, but you're lucky. None come near your camp.

One day, while you're fishing, something strange happens. The water begins to shimmer. It almost glows. Suddenly the reflection in the water is of another world. Your world! You shout for Jasmine and Eduardo, who rush to your side.

"It's home!" Jasmine shouts, then dives in.

Turn the page.

Just like that, she's gone. You and Eduardo are close behind. You dive into the cool water. When you emerge, the Jurassic is gone. It's replaced by familiar sights, sounds, and smells—buildings, car engines, and exhaust. You're on the side of a road. You don't know where you are exactly. But you know *when* you are. You can't wait to get back home.

THE END

To follow another path, turn to page 119.
To learn more about the Jurassic Period, turn to page 211.

You dare not venture out alone. This is home now. A few more years pass when Jasmine falls seriously ill with a fever.

"It was probably something she ate," Eduardo says. "Or something in the water."

Jasmine grows worse by the hour. With no modern medicine, there's nothing you can do for your friend but try to comfort her. She passes away in her sleep.

A month later, Eduardo goes out to collect food. He doesn't return. You go out to search for him the next day with no luck. As you're calling his name, something large stirs in the forest. You hear a roar.

You do the only thing you can. You run. Amazingly, you scramble back to your cave before the beast catches you.

You don't even know what kind of dinosaur it was. This is your life now. The rest of your days, however few they may be, will be spent as prey. And if the predators don't get you, starvation, dehydration, or illness will.

THE END

To follow another path, turn to page 119.
To learn more about the Jurassic Period, turn to page 211.

CHAPTER 3
THE OPEN PLAINS

"This way," you say, moving to the open prairie. "At least out here we'll be able to see anything big coming our way.

The plains seem to stretch on forever. Far in the distance, you can see a herd of some sort of dinosaurs grazing. "I think those are Stegosauruses," Eduardo says with excitement.

"Then let's steer clear," Jasmine suggests. "I don't want to be a Stegosaurus's lunch."

Eduardo laughs. "Don't be silly. They're herbivores. They wouldn't eat you any more than cows would eat you back home."

"Then let's go get a Stegosaurus burger," Jasmine jokes. "I'm hungry."

Turn the page.

Jasmine suddenly freezes. "What's that?" she says.

At first you don't see anything. Then something bursts out from the tall ferns. For a moment, you think it's a crow. It's about that size, and it's covered with feathers. But it's no crow. It looks like some crazy cross between a reptile and a bird.

"Archaeopteryx!" Eduardo squeals with delight.

"Well if I can't have a burger, I'll settle for some Jurassic chicken," Jasmine says.

"What?" Eduardo gasps with dismay. "How could you even think of it?"

"We need to eat," Jasmine answers.

The dinosaur looks at you curiously.

To try to hunt the Archaeopteryx, go to the next page.
To follow it, turn to page 161.

"Jasmine is right," you say. "We should take food when we can get it."

Eduardo looks at you both with disgust. He won't be any help.

"Jasmine, try to draw its attention," you say, "I'll grab it."

Jasmine starts to dance around, while you creep behind the dinosaur. You inch closer. You lunge, wrapping your arms around the animal. It lets out a screech and tries to break free. It's strong for its size, but you hold on tight. That's when it twists its neck and bites your hand.

You scream. The creature's powerful jaws clamp down on your fingers as your skin tears. Suddenly Jasmine dives at it. The little dinosaur lets go of your hand and darts back into the ferns.

Turn the page.

"Well that didn't go well," Eduardo says with a smirk.

"OK, OK. Let's not attack any more dinosaurs for a while," you agree.

Jasmine rips a strip of fabric from the bottom of her T-shirt and wraps your bleeding hand.

"Do you need a break, or are you ready to keep going?" Eduardo asks.

To press on in search of food and shelter, turn to page 170.

To find a place to rest, turn to page 180.

"No way," you whisper. "Did you see those sharp little teeth? Let's see where it goes."

You follow the strange creature as it wanders the open plains. Finally, it leads you back to a nest with six eggs.

"Jackpot!" Jasmine says.

When the dinosaur wanders away again, you grab three of the eggs. Eduardo piles some dry brush and focuses sunlight with his glasses, starting a small fire. You cook the eggs in the shells, then crack them open.

"Not bad," Jasmine says.

"I've been thinking," Eduardo says as he finishes his egg. "We got sent back here when we were imagining the Jurassic. Remember, we put our hands on the Stegosaurus skeleton? What if repeating that might bring us home?"

Turn the page.

"Worth a shot," Jasmine says. "Close your eyes. Imagine home."

You try to picture the museum in as much detail as you can. But when you open your eyes, you're still stuck in a prairie, 150 million years in the past.

"Maybe the Stegosaurus was the key," Jasmine jokes. Eduardo laughs.

But the comment gets you thinking. What if that *was* the key to whatever happened? Could you reproduce the effect?

To try to find somewhere safe to spend the night, turn the page.

To go in search of a Stegosaurus, turn to page 167.

"We need to be serious," you say. "The sun sets in a few hours. We don't want to be out here in the open when it does. We've got to find somewhere safe."

The prairie stretches on in every direction for what feels like forever. As exhaustion sets in, the three of you move along, single file, without speaking. The prospects for shelter are few.

"There are a few large rocks over there," Eduardo says. "We could hunker down there."

Jasmine points to a bushy tree on the horizon.

"We could climb to one of the higher limbs, out of reach of the predators."

The idea of sleeping in a tree isn't very appealing. But then, neither is being eaten by a dinosaur.

To head for the tree, go to the next page.
To take shelter by the rocks, turn to page 171.

You nod your head in agreement with Jasmine. "The tree seems like our best bet."

The sunset blazes brilliant orange by the time you reach the tree.

"I'll take this limb," Jasmine says, claiming the biggest, straightest limb.

You and Eduardo try to get comfortable in twisted crooks in the tree. It's a miserable night. A full moon shines brightly on the open plain.

"Is it just me, or does the moon seem bigger here?" Jasmine asks.

She's right. You'd swear the moon was bigger—or closer—here in the Jurassic. The moonlight shows the dark shapes of predators roaming the open plain. One of them approaches the tree.

"Allosaurus," Eduardo whispers. "Predator."

Turn the page.

Thankfully, you're far out of its reach, and it moves on.

"I'm *not* doing that again," Jasmine says as the three of you climb down in the morning. "Let's go find a Stegosaurus."

"Don't be ridiculous," you argue. "Last night proved how badly we need to find shelter.

Eduardo gives you a shrug. "Sorry, I'm with Jasmine. Let's go."

You watch as they head off in search of a Stegosaurus.

"Are you coming or what?" Jasmine calls.

To go with them, go to the next page.
To split up and continue the search for shelter, turn to page 174.

None of this makes sense. Why shouldn't you go in search of a Stegosaurus? It's as good a plan as any, and you can keep your eyes open for shelter while you look for a herd.

As the three of you move across the open plain, you try to process what has happened to you. None of this should be possible. How could a Stegosaurus fossil send you back in time? A squeal of delight from Jasmine interrupts your thoughts.

"There they are!" she cries.

There are hundreds of them. The Stegosauruses remind you of the bison you once saw at Yellowstone National Park. As you draw close to several stragglers in the herd, you begin to have second thoughts. These animals are *huge*. They're covered with sharp-looking plates. The ground shakes as they move across the plain.

Turn the page.

"Let's go!" Jasmine says. "Look, there's a smaller one. Let's all put our hands on it and think of home."

Smaller is a relative term. The Stegosaurus still dwarfs even the largest bison. If it gets spooked, you'll all be prehistoric pancakes.

To go ahead with the plan, turn to page 176.
To keep your distance, turn to page 179.

There's no time for rest. You strike out across the open plain. You come upon a river. It has carved deep cliffs in the landscape, leaving a steep, rocky bank.

"This is limestone," Eduardo says. "There might be caves. It could be a perfect spot to take shelter."

You spend the rest of the day searching for caves. Jasmine spots one halfway down a particularly steep cliff.

"That would be the perfect place to take shelter," Eduardo says. "But I'm not sure we could make the climb. Falling to our deaths isn't really any better than becoming a dinosaur snack."

"I'm willing to take my chances," Jasmine says. They both look to you.

To look for a better spot, turn to page 183.
To make the climb, turn to page 184.

The rocks don't offer much shelter. But at least you don't have to worry about falling out of a tree in your sleep. The three of you collapse to the ground, backs against the rocks. You're all exhausted. You can only hope you'll be safe here.

After the sun sets, a full moon shines down on the open plains. A scratching sound from the ferns sets your heart racing. You scan the horizon, searching for the shape of some great predator. But there's nothing. Then, out of the brush, something emerges. It's a dinosaur, but it's tiny—not much bigger than a house cat. You let out a breath.

"Hey little guy," you call out softly.

The little dinosaur locks its gaze on you. It takes a careful step forward. Then another. You watch with curiosity. That curiosity turns to terror as another emerges. And another.

Turn the page.

Soon, you're surrounded by the tiny beasts. One of them seemed cute. But dozens of them suddenly are terrifying. And when they charge, you have nowhere to run.

The little dinosaurs, which Eduardo would have told you were Compsognathuses, are lightning-quick, strong, and ferocious. As you face your doom, you can't help but feel cheated. At least if you were going to be eaten by a dinosaur, it could have been a big, terrible lizard. Dying at the hands of a pack of little ones just seems so unfair.

THE END

To follow another path, turn to page 119.
To learn more about the Jurassic Period, turn to page 211.

You won't be a part of this. Maybe if you just strike off in the opposite direction, they'll see that you're right. They'll follow you.

But they don't. And by the time you have second thoughts, they've disappeared into the prairie. They're gone, and you're alone.

You're faster and more efficient on your own. You find eggs and seeds to eat. A rushing brook gives you fresh water.

Days turn to weeks. The flat plains slowly give way to rocky land. It provides plenty of nooks and crannies that offer shelter. As you travel, you see countless dinosaurs. Great herds of armored Stegosauruses and giant Brachiosauruses graze on ferns and brush. You steer clear of the terrible Allosauruses, Ceratosauruses, and other meat eaters.

You make your home on a cliff along a rushing river. You fish. You even learn to set traps for small mammals and dinosaurs. Somehow you survive and grow old. Your hair slowly turns gray.

One day, when you're foraging, you spot something far in the distance. It's a *human*!

You run. You shout. It must be one of your friends, after all these years. But the person is too far away. He or she doesn't see you. By the time you reach the ridge, there's no one there.

You'd assumed Jasmine and Eduardo had died. But now your heart is filled with hope. You will not rest until you find whomever it was you saw in the distance. Maybe you won't have to spend your final years alone after all.

THE END

To follow another path, turn to page 119.
To learn more about the Jurassic Period, turn to page 211.

You've come this far, why stop now? You take a deep breath and follow Jasmine. Eduardo is right behind you.

The Stegosaurus is munching on some low ferns. If it notices you approaching, it doesn't seem to mind. Now that you're close to it, the size of the beast truly astounds you. It's more than twice your height, and as long as a bus. Jasmine places her hand on the animal's huge rear leg. It doesn't stir. Eduardo does the same. They both look back at you, waiting.

"Here goes nothing," you mutter under your breath, reaching out your hand.

The animal's hide is rough and leathery. It's warmer than you expected. You close your eyes and imagine home. You concentrate on places and people, imagining what it's like to live in your time.

Turn the page.

Suddenly you feel a familiar sense of dizziness. You start to fall and then pass out. When you wake, you're on the floor of the museum. The Stegosaurus skeleton towers over you.

Your mind is fuzzy. You have strange memories of a distant place and strange adventures. Jasmine and Eduardo sit up and rub their eyes.

"Did that really just happen?" you ask.

The three of you catch up with your class in the Ancient Egypt exhibit. By the time you leave the museum, you've almost forgotten all of it, like a dream fading away with morning light.

Was it real? As the years pass, you're not sure. Maybe it was your imagination. Or just maybe, you had one of the strangest adventures of all time.

THE END

To follow another path, turn to page 119.
To learn more about the Jurassic Period, turn to page 211.

"This is a bad idea," you say, backing away.

As you move, you stumble over a rock and let out a yelp. The sound spooks the Stegosaurus. It lumbers forward. Eduardo tries to dodge the beast, but it swats him with its massive tail.

The blow sends Eduardo's limp body flying. Jasmine screams. The dinosaur whips its tail again, now in her direction. You can only watch in horror.

Just like that, you're all alone. The herd moves on, leaving your friends lifeless on the ground.

You never do go home. Somehow you survive into old age. Your life in the Jurassic is difficult and lonely. There are times you almost wish the Stegosaurus had gotten you too.

THE END

To follow another path, turn to page 119.
To learn more about the Jurassic Period, turn to page 211.

Your hand is throbbing.

"I think I might throw up," you say with a grimace. "I need to rest."

You quickly drift off to sleep. You awaken with a start. Jasmine is screaming. Eduardo is tugging on your shirt. The sight of a towering dinosaur looming over you reminds you very quickly where . . . and when . . . you are.

"Allosaurus!" Eduardo shouts.

Your friends are running, but the Allosaurus is gaining on them.

"Ed! Jasmine!" you shout.

Without even thinking about it, you rush after them, toward the dinosaur.

"Hey!" you shout at the beast, waving your arms in the air.

Turn the page.

You just want to distract it long enough to let your friends escape. But then the dinosaur turns on you. It covers the open ground between you with blinding speed. There's nowhere to hide. It's too fast. As you frantically try to zig and zag out of its path, you can feel its hot breath. Its jaws open wide. It strikes.

You've given your life for your friends. You just hope they took the chance you gave them to get away.

THE END

To follow another path, turn to page 119.
To learn more about the Jurassic Period, turn to page 211.

Ed is right. The climb down might be more dangerous than taking your chances up here.

"Keep going," you decide. "If there's one cave, there should be more."

The sun dips low in the sky as you search.

"There's just nothing here," Jasmine says with exasperation. "We're running out of time."

Dusk turns to dark. When the predators come, Eduardo can't even tell you what the horse-sized dinosaurs are. There's not enough time. The pack surrounds you, cutting off any avenue of escape.

You only wish you'd tried to take shelter in the cave. Three humans, exposed on the open plains of the Jurassic at night, never had a chance.

THE END

To follow another path, turn to page 119.
To learn more about the Jurassic Period, turn to page 211.

The climb is treacherous. But so is your current situation. Jasmine lowers herself down, grasping plant roots for support, until she reaches the small opening. Then she disappears inside. A minute later she sticks out her head, smiling.

"It's perfect!" she says. "Come on down."

You follow her route, almost slipping once and tumbling to your death. But you hold on, and so does Eduardo. You collapse into a cozy cave, just the right size for the three of you.

"Welcome to our new home," Jasmine says.

The cave is damp and narrow. But you'll be safe from predators here.

"We'll use those roots to make a ladder," Jasmine says. "We can go down to fish and up to forage for food. We can survive here!"

All thoughts of trying to get home have disappeared. The reality of your situation has sunk in. The Jurassic is where you live now. You're just glad you have your friends with you. You don't think you could make it alone. Together, you have a chance to survive.

THE END

To follow another path, turn to page 119.
To learn more about the Jurassic Period, turn to page 211.

"Let's keep moving on foot," you suggest. "We'll see how it goes. We can always change our minds if it's not going well."

The three of you trudge through the swamp, often wading through waist-deep water. You detour away from the river bank when Eduardo spots a strip of higher, dryer land. It's there that you spot a nest. It's a huge bowl of mud, nestled near some tree roots. And it's filled with eggs. Enormous eggs.

"Could be supper," Jasmine suggests.

"I'd hate to run into whatever laid those eggs, though," Eduardo replies.

To leave the nest alone, go to the next page.
To try to gather some eggs, turn to page 198.

"Whatever laid those eggs could be close by," you say, backing away. "No, I think we'll leave those eggs right where they are."

You continue, following the river as it meanders through the swamp. Your feet stick in the mud with every step. Your legs are getting tired.

You notice some giant footprints in the wet ground. It almost looks like something bulldozed a path through this part of the swamp.

You hear the animal before you see it. Its low groan sends shivers down your spine. When you finally catch sight of it, though, Eduardo says you don't have to be afraid.

"It's a Diplodocus!" he says with excitement, "A plant eater."

Turn the page

Life is hard. You endure terrible storms, food shortages, and illness. But somehow you make it. You and your friends carve out a life.

"This just isn't enough," Jasmine decides one day. "We need to move on and explore. What's the point of living in the Jurassic if we can't see everything? Who knows, we might even find a way home."

You try to change her mind, but she's set in her decision. She's leaving. Eduardo refuses. He's staying. Like it or not, your little group is going to split up.

To stay on the beach with Eduardo, turn to page 204.
To explore the world with Jasmine, turn to page 209.

You're not going to survive long unless you eat something. You scan the ground for any sign of whatever laid those eggs, but you don't see anything.

"Here goes nothing," you say as you carefully approach the nest.

The eggs are oblong, more oval than a chicken egg, and much bigger. As you scoop one up, it feels almost soft to the touch. You tuck it under one arm like a football, then scoop up another. As you turn around, you hear a rustling from the trees above.

"Look out!" Eduardo calls.

Just then something massive drops from the trees. It's a snake! You once saw a giant anaconda at the zoo. This massive creature makes it seem tiny.

The snake wraps itself around you, coiling its body around and around. Eduardo and Jasmine try to save you, but they can't pry the snake loose. It starts to squeeze. The air rushes from your lungs. You hear the sound of your ribs cracking. Then everything goes black.

THE END

To follow another path, turn to page 119.
To learn more about the Jurassic Period, turn to page 211.

Ed is right. Even plant-eating dinosaurs of this size are a threat. You'll have to find another way.

You swing around the herd, putting some distance between you and the giant Diplodocuses. You're feeling good about your choice until you see a different kind of dinosaur—a meat-eating Ceratosaurus. It looks a little like the T. rexes you've seen in movies, walking upright on two hind legs. Razor-sharp teeth gleam from its open jaws.

The Ceratosaurus is big, fast, and hungry. You run as fast as you can, but it's not fast enough.

In the last moment before it snatches you up, you shout, "Keep running!"

Maybe your friends will escape your terrible fate.

THE END

To follow another path, turn to page 119.
To learn more about the Jurassic Period, turn to page 211.

"These guys are huge. Predators are going to keep their distance," you decide. "Let's take our chances with the herd."

The herd moves slowly along the bank. You stay close, and no predators come near. The dinosaurs mostly ignore you. They seem content to let you tag along.

Several days pass. After about a week with the herd, you head out in search of food. That's when you see something remarkable. You come upon a still pool of crystal-clear water. Thinking it might be a spring, you approach it. What you see beneath the surface takes your breath away. The reflection in the pool is home! You can see familiar plants, roads, and even buildings in the reflection. Could this be some portal back to your time? Your heart races with excitement.

"Hey!" you shout. "Come here!"

"Could it be a way home?" Ed asks.

You do the only thing you can. You dive into the cold water. When you return to the surface, everything has changed. You're back in your own time. Soaking wet, the three of you trudge through familiar plants and trees until you come to a highway. Your city is in the distance.

"What will we tell people?" Jasmine asks.

You've been asking yourself the same question. No one will believe you. That's when you remember your phone.

"If my memory card is still good, I've got some photographs that are going to make us famous," you say with a smile.

THE END

To follow another path, turn to page 119.
To learn more about the Jurassic Period, turn to page 211.

"This is the only place I've felt even a little bit safe since we came here," you tell Jasmine. "How can we leave it?"

She just shakes her head. She's determined to go off alone, and you can't stop her. You and Eduardo watch as she disappears around a bend in the shoreline. You're afraid you'll never see her again.

Life on the beach grows routine. You do the same things to survive, day after day. Your blazing campfire usually keeps the dinosaurs away.

Years pass. One day, Eduardo goes to collect wood for the fire. He doesn't return. You search for your friend but find no trace. He may have fallen prey to an Allosaurus, Ceratosaurus, or some other predator.

Turn the page.

You're all alone. Life was hard and repetitive even when you had company. Now, all alone, it's unbearable. You fall into depression. You stop maintaining your campfire. And the predators notice. When a pack of dog-sized dinosaurs strikes, you try climbing a small tree. But with a CRACK, the tree's trunk snaps. As you crash to the ground, you know what awaits. The small dinosaurs are about to get a taste of the future.

THE END

To follow another path, turn to page 119.
To learn more about the Jurassic Period, turn to page 211.

With monsters like that lurking below the muddy water, there's no way you can stay on this little raft.

"Let's get to land," you say.

The others nod their heads in agreement. You steer your raft to the other shore, far from where you saw the giant croc. It feels good to step back onto land. It's not so swampy here. You've floated into rockier, drier land.

For the next two days, you make your way on foot, drinking from small streams and eating mushrooms and seeds. Eduardo gets sick first. His stomach is cramping badly, and he can't keep anything down. You and Jasmine soon suffer from the same illness.

"Probably something in the water," Eduardo moans. "A bacteria or a parasite."

Turn the page.

Within a day, Eduardo is delirious. You're all burning up with a terrible fever. You suffer from extreme chills. There's nowhere to go for help and no one coming to your aid. You thought meat-eating dinosaurs were the biggest danger in this time period, but it turns out the microscopic life in the Jurassic is every bit as deadly.

THE END

To follow another path, turn to page 119.
To learn more about the Jurassic Period, turn to page 211.

You can't let Jasmine go alone. Eduardo has everything he needs to survive here. You pack some dried fish, and head out with Jasmine along the coast. As you round a bend, you take one last long look at Eduardo. Will you ever see him again?

You and Jasmine see amazing things. You escape packs of small, speedy theropods. You are nearly swallowed up by a sinkhole. Jasmine rides an Apatosaurus. You travel the world, seeing creatures that will one day be lost to history.

It's the adventure of a lifetime, but through it all, you never stop dreaming of home and your family. You'll never see them again. You understand that now. One day, you'll return to the beach. You just hope Eduardo is still there to welcome you.

THE END

To follow another path, turn to page 119.
To learn more about the Jurassic Period, turn to page 211.

CHAPTER 5

THE JURASSIC PERIOD

The Jurassic Period was at the heart of the Mesozoic Era. This era is known as the Age of Reptiles. The Jurassic spanned about 55 million years, starting at the end of the Triassic Period about 201 million years ago.

The Jurassic Period was the time when dinosaurs rose up to dominate life on Earth. Giant Diplodocus, measuring 100 feet long, ate plant life. Deadly Allosaurus hunted small prey. Spiky Stegosaurus roamed the land in large herds. Pterosaurs soared through the skies. Marine reptiles such as plesiosaurs swam in the seas. Meanwhile, the earliest birds appeared during this time, having evolved from dinosaurs.

The Jurassic was marked by major changes in Earth's geology. It saw the breakup of the supercontinent Pangaea, which split into two main landmasses, called Laurasia and Gondwanaland. The opening of seaways about 145 million years ago marked the end of the Jurassic and the beginning of a new period, the Cretaceous.

Dinosaurs and other reptiles continued to rule the planet during that period. It ended about 65 million years ago with a mass extinction that wiped out the dinosaurs and many other life forms on Earth. Scientists have found evidence of a large asteroid strike that likely caused this extinction. It knocked reptiles from their rule and paved the way for an age of more adaptable mammals to begin.

TIMELINE

252 million years ago•••

Paleozoic Era
time of ancient life

Mesozoic Era
time of dinosaurs

251 ••••••••••••••••••200
million years ago   million years ago
TRIASSIC PERIOD

200 ••••••••••••••••••••••••••••••
million years ago
JURASSIC PERIOD

252 MILLION YEARS AGO
A mass extinction marks the end of the Paleozoic Era, sparking a rapid change in animal and plant life. The Mesozoic Era begins, with the first of its three periods, the Triassic. The age of reptiles begins.

210-200 MILLION YEARS AGO
Triassic Period ends, and Jurassic begins.

180 MILLION YEARS AGO
The Atlantic Ocean and Indian Ocean form as the supercontinent Pangaea breaks apart.

230-220 MILLION YEARS AGO
The first dinosaurs appear.

201 MILLION YEARS AGO
The supercontinent Pangaea begins to break up, causing rapid changes to the planet's climate and setting off a large extinction event. This marks the end of the Triassic Period and the beginning of the Jurassic. The planet's climate is warm and wet, supporting a wide variety of life.

· ·•65 million years ago

Cenozoic Era
time of mammals

· · · · · · · · · · · ·•146
million years ago

145 ·•65
million years ago   million years ago
CRETACEOUS PERIOD

145 MILLION YEARS AGO
The Jurassic Period ends, giving way to the Cretaceous Period. Dinosaurs such as Tyrannosaurus rex and Triceratops roam the Earth during the Cretaceous.

65 MILLION YEARS AGO
A massive asteroid strike drastically changes Earth's climate. Large reptiles such as dinosaurs are unable to adapt to the rapidly changing conditions, leading to a mass extinction. The Cretaceous Period and the Mesozoic Era end. The Cenozoic Era begins. It is the Age of Mammals.

150 MILLION YEARS AGO
Archaeopteryx appears in the fossil record. Among the many kinds of feathered dinosaurs, scientists recognize it as the earliest bird.

80 MILLION YEARS AGO
North America separates from Europe, completing the breakup of Pangaea.

Pangaea

COULD YOU SURVIVE THE ICE AGE?

BY BLAKE HOENA

ILLUSTRATED BY ALESSANDRO VALDRIGHI

TABLE OF CONTENTS

INTRODUCTION

YOU are an ordinary kid going about your everyday life. Suddenly you find yourself in a strange place and a strange time. It's a period from long ago. The world looks different than anything you've ever seen before. Terrifying beasts roam the land. Danger lurks at every turn. Where will you find shelter? How will you get food? Will you ever see your friends and family again? Most importantly of all, can you survive?

Chapter One sets the scene. Then you choose which path to take. Follow the directions at the bottom of each page. The choices you make determine what happens next. After you finish your path, go back and read the others for more adventures.

YOU CHOOSE the path you take through the Ice Age!

Turn the page to begin your adventure.

CHAPTER 1

THE MUSEUM OF NATURAL HISTORY

You and your classmates are headed to a class trip at the Museum of Natural History.

"I can't wait to see what they have on display," your friend Jayla says.

"I'm just excited to get out of class today," Mateo jokes.

You and Jayla roll your eyes.

Mr. Andrist stands at the front of the bus.

"OK, students," he says, "once we get off the bus, a museum guide will lead you through exhibits of the Pleistocene Epoch."

Turn the page.

You have already learned in class that this period of Earth's history started about 2.5 million years ago. It marked the beginning of the last Ice Age and lasted until about 12,000 years ago.

In Mr. Andrist's class, you have studied animals called megafauna that lived during the Pleistocene Epoch. Many were giant versions of modern-day animals, such as the cave bear and the saber-toothed cat. This time period is also when modern-day humans evolved.

When Mr. Andrist stops talking, your classmates file off the bus. In front of the museum's glass doors stands a young woman with a name tag that reads "Rebecca."

"Hello! I am one of the paleontologists on staff at the museum," she says. "Does everyone know what a paleontologist does?"

"You study old things," Mateo says.

The students around you chuckle quietly.

"Well, yes," Rebecca says. "Though, here at the museum, I also get to share my knowledge with budding scientists such as yourselves."

Rebecca shows you displays of Ice Age people and animals. You learn that in Europe, Neanderthals went extinct about 40,000 years ago, shortly after modern-day humans called Cro-Magnons arrived. Camels called camelops roamed western parts of North America. Australia had giant crocodiles and lizards.

After lunch, you line up in a long hallway. You scoot to the front with Jayla and Mateo. There are three doorways with a sign above each one. One sign says, "North America," another reads, "Europe," and the last reads, "Australia."

Turn the page.

"This ends the guided part of your tour," Rebecca says. "But your adventure isn't over yet."

She goes on to explain that you are going to learn about the last glacial period, which began almost 100,000 years ago and ended about 12,000 years ago. During this time in North America, glaciers covered most of Canada and extended south into the United States. Northern parts of Europe and Asia were also covered in these mountain-sized sheets of slow-moving ice. Even Australia was affected by the cold temperatures.

"At the end of this hallway are three doorways," she adds. "Each one holds an exhibit about a different part of the world. Go ahead and explore, but please don't touch the artifacts. They are very old and fragile." Rebecca pauses before adding, "And some are rather special."

Jayla turns to you and Mateo and asks, "Which one should we check out?"

"It doesn't matter to me," Mateo says.

Both friends look to you to decide.

To go to the North American display, turn the page.
To go to the European display, turn to page 259.
To go to the Australian display, turn to page 283.

CHAPTER 2

NORTH AMERICA

You point to the doorway with the sign that says "North America."

"Let's check out how things were in North America," you say.

"Yeah, it'd be cool to know if glaciers reached where we live," Jayla says.

Just before reaching the doorway, you see a map of North America on the wall. Jayla leans in to read a plaque below the map.

"It says the last glacial period reached its peak about 20,000 to 25,000 years ago," she says. "During this time, the Laurentide and Cordilleran Ice Sheets covered most of Canada and parts of the United States."

Turn the page.

The doorway opens up into a large exhibit of a scene from prehistoric times. There is a woolly mammoth and a saber-toothed cat. You and your friends wander over to a diorama of a village of Clovis people. They are believed to be some of the first people to live in North America. In front of the display, you notice something odd on the ground. It looks like a spear dropped from one of the figures in the diorama. The three of you all seem to be drawn to the spear. You know you're not supposed to, but you bend down to pick it up at the same time.

As you touch the spear, you feel a slight tingle in your fingers. Then a cool breeze wraps around you. You shiver.

"Did you feel that?" Jayla asks.

"Brrr," Mateo says. "It feels like we are in the Ice Age."

You look back at your friends and are surprised to see them standing on the edge of a rocky cliff. A river rages beneath it.

"I think we are!" you blurt out in shock. You glance around at your new surroundings and feel a cold gust tousle your hair.

"What happened to the museum?" Mateo cries out in fear.

"I don't know," Jayla answers, nervously. "But I know I want to get down from here!"

To your right the ground slopes into flat plains as far as the eye can see. To your left the ground rolls into grassy hills with brush and trees dotted throughout.

To head toward the plains, turn the page.
To wander into the rolling hills, turn to page 233.

"It will probably be easier to walk in the flatlands," you say. "Let's go right."

For a while, it's easy going, if a bit boring. But after an hour or so, the ground behind you begins to rumble.

"What's that?" Mateo asks. "An earthquake?"

"Worse," Jayla answers. "Mammoths!"

You spin around to see a group of woolly mammoths with shaggy fur and incredibly long tusks trotting your way.

"We really are in the Ice Age!" you exclaim.

The lead mammoth raises its head and lets out a deafening sound through its trunk.

"I don't think it likes us," you whisper.

The mammoth trumpets again and takes another step forward.

Turn the page.

"It's going to charge," Jayla says.

"What should we do?" Mateo asks.

You could turn and run. Running might make a predator think you are prey. But mammoths are plant eaters. You doubt it would chase you. Or would it? Maybe you should stand your ground. Waving your arms and making noise can scare off some animals.

To turn and run, turn to page 236.
To stand your ground, turn to page 237.

"The hills seem safer," you say. "We can hide from predators there. Let's go left.

You walk on for about an hour, when Jayla suddenly gasps. Lurking in the grass in front of you is a large cat with two very long canine teeth. It snarls menacingly.

"Oh no," Mateo whispers as he gulps in fear. "Is that a saber-toothed cat?"

"It sure looks like one," Jayla says.

The cat crouches back on its haunches and growls. You know that saber-toothed cats are carnivores, just like modern-day big cats. They eat other animals for food. You now realize that not only can you hide from predators in the hills, they can hide from you too.

"What do we do?" Jayla asks.

Turn the page.

You could make a run for it, hoping that people aren't part of a saber-toothed cat's diet. Or you can stand your ground, hoping that three kids are too threatening for the cat to risk attacking.

To stand your ground, turn to page 241.
To turn and run, turn to page 245.

Woolly mammoths, like modern-day elephants, eat plants, not animals. The mammoth wouldn't think of you as prey, so you turn and run.

"Come on!" you yell to your friends.

All three of you take off running. What you didn't realize is that by turning your back on the mammoth, you are showing signs of fear. The mammoth trumpets again, and the beasts lumber after you, hoping to drive you off.

You run as fast as you can, but you are no match for the big beasts. Suddenly you feel a tusk swipe at you. You fly into the air. When you crash back to the earth, the wind is knocked out of you. You can't get out of the way as the mammoths trample you to death.

THE END

To follow another path, turn to page 225.
To learn more about the Ice Age, turn to page 314.

You know that it is best not to run from predators. But acting intimidating can actually scare them off. Maybe that would work for a woolly mammoth too.

"Do what I do," you tell your friends. You wave your hands over your head and shout, "No! No! No!" as loud as you can.

"Stop! Stop! Stop!" Jayla yells as she jumps up and down.

"Don't be a woolly bully," Mateo shouts as he waves his arms back and forth.

The mammoth looks like it is not sure about you or what it should do. Then it trumpets one last time before turning and walking away. The rest of the herd follows. You breathe a sigh of relief as they lumber off in the other direction.

"Whew, that was scary," Jayla says.

Turn the page.

"I can't believe we just faced down a herd of woolly mammoths," Mateo says. "No one will believe this."

"If we don't figure out how to get back to the museum, we won't have anyone to tell," you say.

You wonder what to do next. Somehow, you traveled back in time to when woolly mammoths roamed the earth. What other dangers might you run into?

"We should find shelter or water," Jayla says.

Glancing around, you see the sun glinting off what you think might be water in the distance.

"Let's head that way," you say, pointing toward a spot on the horizon. "I think I see water."

After hiking for a time, you reach a wide river. You bend down to scoop up a handful of water to drink.

Turn the page.

After everyone relieves their thirst, Jayla says, "We still need shelter."

"And to find a way home," Mateo adds.

You know that as long as you stay close to the river, you will have water. But to find shelter, and possibly a way back to your own time, you have no idea what to do or where to head. Should you follow the river north or south?

To go north, turn to page 246.
To go south, turn to page 248.

You could never outrun a saber-toothed cat. And if you did run, it might think you are prey and pounce. So you decide to stand your ground and hope that the three of you can scare the cat away.

"Do what I do," you say to your friends.

You raise your arms, trying to look as big as you can. Then you shout at the top of your lungs.

"Get! Shoo! Scram!" Jayla yells as she jumps up and down.

"You big scaredy-cat!" Mateo shouts as he wriggles his arms all about.

The saber-toothed cat stops. It looks unsure about what to do. It growls as you continue to shout and scream, but it slowly slinks backward. You don't stop what you are doing until the cat turns and pads away.

Turn the page.

"Wow, I can't believe that worked," Jayla says.

"No one's gonna mess with us now," Mateo says. "Not even a T. rex."

"Don't worry about that. Dinosaurs went extinct long before the Ice Age," you say.

Now that the present danger is over, you have to figure out what do to next. Somehow, you ended up back during a time when saber-toothed cats lived. You are sure there are other dangerous prehistoric beasts.

"We should seek shelter or maybe find water," Jayla says, and then she points to something off in the distance. "That looks like a river."

You see sunlight glinting off the waves. "Let's head that way."

"As long as we head in the opposite direction as the saber-toothed cat, I'm good," Mateo says.

Turn the page.

You walk for more than an hour before coming to a raging river. There is no way you can swim across. To continue on, you need to follow it to the north or south. Glancing in either direction, all you see is grassland stretching out to the horizon.

"Does it matter which way we go?" Mateo asks.

Jayla looks to the south and then to the north.

"I don't see much of a difference," she adds. "But as long as we stay close to the river, we'll have water.

To turn north, turn to page 246.
To turn south, turn to page 248.

You don't want to stick around to find out if Ice Age cat food includes humans. It's best to run.

"Let's make a run for it," you whisper.

Jayla and Mateo both nod. The cat snarls again and paws at the ground.

"Go!" you shout.

You, Mateo, and Jayla make a break for it. What you didn't realize is that by running, the saber-toothed cat thinks you're prey. You don't get very far before you feel it slam you to the ground. Then two sharp, knifelike teeth dig into your neck and shoulder. The saber-toothed cat quickly ends your life.

THE END

To follow another path, turn to page 225.
To learn more about the Ice Age, turn to page 314.

You don't know where you are, so one direction seems as good as another.

"Then let's head this way," you say, turning north. You follow the river as it winds north.

Hiking along, you rarely see any other animals, and you don't see any other people. As the days pass, your feet and legs grow sore. The grumbling of your stomach reminds you how hungry you are. But in the end, it is not prehistoric beasts or hunger that leads to your downfall. The farther you travel north, the colder the temperatures get.

Then one day, you see a mountainous cliff of ice blocking your path. It is then that you realize the river you had been following was created by glacier water.

"That glacier must be miles thick," Jayla says.

"I can't go any farther," Mateo says, dropping to his knees.

"It was a mistake to come this way," you mumble to yourself.

You realize you should have been traveling south, away from the glaciers. You rest under the shadow of the looming mountain of ice. That night, a storm rolls in. The area is blanketed in snow. You and your friends huddle together for warmth. But it does little good. Everyone is shivering violently. Hypothermia sets in as your body temperature drops. Slowly, each of you drifts off to sleep, never to wake again.

THE END

To follow another path, turn to page 225.
To learn more about the Ice Age, turn to page 314.

"Let's head south," you say. "If this is the Ice Age, we don't want to head north. That's where the glaciers are."

"Makes sense to me," Mateo says.

Your group turns south, following the river. You have water to drink whenever you are thirsty. But you are unsure about eating any of the berries or plants you see. They could be poisonous. Soon your stomachs are grumbling.

"Let's take a break," Mateo says after a while. "I'm beat."

You have no idea where you are or where you are going. What's the harm in stopping?

"OK," you say.

All three of you are tired, sweaty, and hungry. You flop to the ground.

"Ouch," Mateo shouts, swatting at a bug. "These prehistoric mosquitoes are huge!"

"Quiet, I think I hear something," Jayla says.

The three of you quietly listen. Over the sound of the water and the buzz of insects, you think you hear voices.

"It's people," Mateo says.

"We should go investigate," Jayla says.

You walk quietly in the direction of the voices. You keep your heads down and duck behind bushes as you creep along. Then you crawl up a hill and peek over the top of it.

In the distance you see a large fire in the middle of a small village. The shelters look somewhat like Native American tepees, but they seem to be built out of plant materials.

Turn the page.

"They might be Neanderthals," Mateo says.

"No, they lived in Europe, not North America," Jayla says.

"Those are the Clovis," you say. "Like the people in the diorama back at the museum."

You don't know much about these ancient people. You certainly won't understand their language, and you don't know if they're friendly. Maybe it would be safest to avoid them. But then, you don't have any food, shelter, or a means to start a fire. The people in the village have everything you need.

To avoid the village, turn the page.
To go meet the people, turn to page 254.

You barely survived an encounter with a dangerous prehistoric animal. You don't think it's worth the risk of meeting prehistoric people. They may not be any friendlier than the beast you faced.

"It looks like they have food," Mateo says hopefully.

"But look, they also have weapons," you say, pointing to their spears.

Mateo and Jayla nod in agreement. The three of you sneak back down the hill and quietly make your way along the river. You are careful not to be seen or heard by the people of the village.

While you are able to avoid other people and large animals, you are constantly struggling to feed yourself. You spend almost all of your time looking for food.

The days turn into weeks and the weeks into months. Slowly you give up on ever returning back to the museum or seeing your classmates and family again. You and your friends spend the rest of your lives just trying to survive the harsh environment of the Ice Age.

THE END

To follow another path, turn to page 225.
To learn more about the Ice Age, turn to page 314.

"I think we should check out the village," you say. "The people there can't be worse than facing a saber-toothed cat or a woolly mammoth."

"And I'm hungry," Mateo says.

"Plus they have a fire," Jayla adds.

"I don't think we have any other choice," you say.

The three of you begin walking toward the village. Soon you hear yelling. Several men armed with spears come running toward you. They shout at you in a language you don't understand. You and your friends do your best to keep calm.

You raise your hands in front of you and quietly say, "We mean you no harm."

"We are cold," Jayla says, pointing to the fire.

"And hungry," Mateo says, motioning with one hand toward his open mouth.

Turn the page.

After a few tense moments, the prehistoric people stop shouting and shaking their spears at you. One man waves you forward toward the fire, where you take a seat. A little while later, a woman brings each of you a bowl of food. She motions by bringing her hand to her mouth.

"She wants us to eat," Jayla says.

"What is it?" Mateo asks, looking at his bowl.

You are too hungry to care. It's food, and you're starving. As you eat, one of the men squats down next to you. He sets his spear on the ground between you and your friends. You all look at it and then at each other with a shock of familiarity. It certainly looks like the spear you touched at the museum. At the same time, all three of you reach over and touch it. Suddenly you feel a familiar tingle. The air shimmers around you.

In an instant, the crackle of the fire is replaced by the excited voices of your friends.

"We're back!" Mateo exclaims.

You find yourself in the museum standing next to the fallen spear. Just then, Rebecca walks by. She takes a pair of gloves out of her pocket and puts them on. Then she bends down to pick up the spear.

"This is one of those special artifacts," she says, with a wink. "I'd better put it somewhere safe."

THE END

To follow another path, turn to page 225.
To learn more about the Ice Age, turn to page 314.

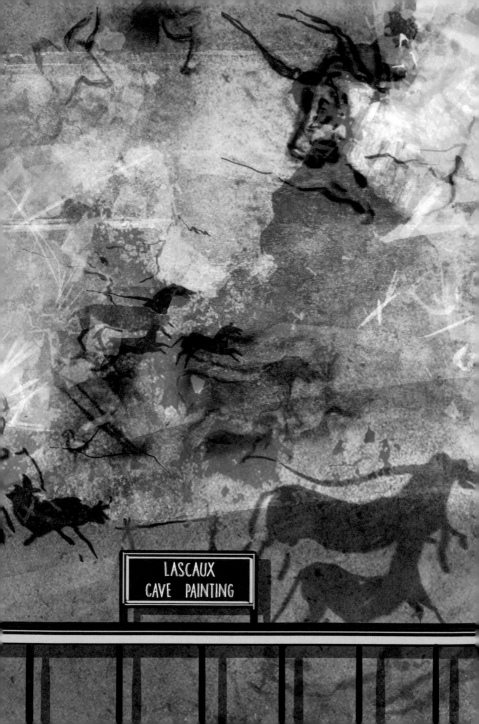

LASCAUX
CAVE PAINTING

CHAPTER 3

EUROPE

"Let's check out Europe," you say. "I want to see what Neanderthals and Cro-Magnon people looked like."

You head toward the Europe display, and your friends follow. As you enter the room, Mateo points to something painted on one wall.

"What are those?" he asks.

"They look like a painting of some sort of animals," you say.

"They're cave paintings," Jayla says. "Like those found in the Lascaux Caves in France."

You walk over to the cave paintings with your friends. You are surprised at how lifelike it looks. The wall appears to be real rock.

Turn the page.

Mesmerized, you and your friends forget about Rebecca's warning and lean in to touch it. You feel a tingle in your fingers. Suddenly you are surrounded by darkness.

"Whoa, what just happened?" Mateo asks. "Are we still in the museum?"

"I don't know," you say, glancing around. "I don't think so."

"It looks like we're in an actual cave!" Jayla exclaims.

"OK, this is weird," Mateo says.

The only light comes from the sun shining through an entrance on the far side of the cave. As your eyes adjust to the dim light, you see paintings on the walls. They are red and black.

"They look real," Jayla says, inspecting them.

On the ground there are bowls filled with what looks like red and black paste. In the middle of the cave are the remains of a fire.

"Let's see what's outside," Mateo says, stepping through the entrance. "This cave is creeping me out."

You and Jayla follow him. Outside is a tundra-like landscape of shrubs and grasses. You don't see any glaciers in the mountainous ridges around you, but you feel the bite of cold air.

"Brr," Jayla says. "It sure feels like we're back in the Ice Age."

You have an odd feeling that she might be right. There is a village a little farther down in the valley. A group of people have gathered below you. They are covered in furs and some carry spears with stone tips. They look shorter and a little more stout than modern-day humans.

Turn the page.

"They might be Cro-Magnons," Jayla explains.

Suddenly Mateo screams. He has stumbled and is tumbling down into the valley.

"Mateo!" you shout.

You and Jayla quickly scramble down after him in a panic. By the time you get to the bottom of the valley, Mateo is surrounded by the strangers. The surprised people are helping him to his feet.

"Are you hurt?" you ask.

"Yeah, just a little bruised," Mateo says. "Thankfully these people seem friendly."

"Maybe they will take us in," Jayla says. "It's probably strange to see three kids wandering alone—especially in these clothes."

A man and a woman approach you. The man offers you a spear while the woman holds out some wooden bowls.

"I think they want us to either go on a hunt or help them find food," you say.

To go on a hunt, turn the page.
To help gather food, turn to page 266.

"It would be exciting to go on a hunt," you say. "Maybe we'll see some prehistoric animals."

You and your friends each grab a spear. The man leads you and a group of hunters to a watering hole. You hide in the brush and wait. Eventually you hear a distant trumpeting sound. You peek through the leaves to see several woolly mammoths heading your way. The ground shakes.

Everyone stays hidden until the beasts get near the watering hole. Then one man lunges forward from his hiding spot and stabs the nearest mammoth. It trumpets angrily and rises up on its hind legs.

The mammoth is vulnerable. It seems like a good time to join in the attack. Or should you wait to see what the other hunters do?

To wait, turn to page 268.
To rush in, turn to page 272.

"I don't know how to use a spear," you say.

"And I'd rather not run into any wild animals," Jayla adds.

Mateo nods in agreement.

Each of you grabs one of the bowls and follows the woman. Some Cro-Magnon children and other women join you.

While everyone else wanders off searching for berries and other edible plants, the woman guides you over to some shrubs. She shows you which berries to pick and which to leave alone.

Time passes, and you are lost in thought as you pick berries off of the bushes. You glance up when you hear a loud huff near you. Staring at you from across a small clearing is the biggest hairy face you have ever seen.

"Hey, Jayla," you whisper. "What is that?"

"A cave bear," she says, already frozen in fear.

The bear steps forward, crushing the shrubs in front of it. It's huge! On all fours, it stands as tall as you. It is stocky, and you guess it weighs as much as a small car.

"What do they eat?" you ask.

"I think they're omnivores," Jayla replies.

While there are plenty of plants around, you and your friends are the only "meat" nearby.

"I hope it's in the mood for a salad," Mateo says.

You need to get away from the bear. You could throw your bowl of fruit down and make a run for it. Hopefully the bear would be more interested in the berries than in you. Or you could set the bowl down and back away slowly.

To throw the berries and run, turn to page 273.
To slowly back away, turn to page 274.

You look at the other hunters. Even though the mammoth has its belly exposed, they don't move in for the kill. They seem to be waiting for something. You should probably follow their lead.

The injured mammoth trumpets angrily again. It drops on all fours and then spins around. The herd flees the waterhole.

You and the other hunters follow in pursuit. Every now and then the herd stops. This gives the hunters a chance to attack the injured animal. They launch spears at it from a safe distance. But for the most part, the men are content to simply follow the herd.

"I think they're hoping to wear it out," Jayla says.

She's right. It takes hours, but eventually the mammoth tires from the constant harassment of the hunters. It is slowed by its injuries and struggles to defend itself. That is when the hunters go in for the kill.

Once the hunt is done, other members of the tribe join you. They help in butchering the beast and preparing the meat and its hide. These tasks take the rest of the day.

By nightfall, you are back in the cave. A fire is lit, and you and your friends huddle around it for warmth.

You look at the wall with the cave paintings.

"Maybe we should paint a scene from the hunt today," you say.

Turn the page.

"There's paint," Jayla says, pointing to the bowls along the wall.

Mateo jumps up and heads over to the wall.

"There are brushes, too," he says, holding up some sticks with hair attached to one end.

You walk over to your friend and grab one of the brushes and the bowl of red paint.

"What are you going to paint?" Jayla asks.

"One of the mammoths," you say.

You dip the brush into the paint. When you touch the wall with it, you feel a familiar tingle in your fingers.

Suddenly it is a lot brighter and noisier. The sounds of your excited classmates surround you. Jayla and Mateo are next to you.

Turn to page 281.

With the mammoth exposing its underside, you see an opportunity to attack and impress the other hunters. You stand up from your hiding spot and lunge forward with your spear. As you do, the mammoth drops back to all fours. While the mammoth may be injured, the huge beast is far from defeated. It takes a swipe at you with its long tusks. You are lifted into the air and tossed to the ground.

As you struggle to get to your feet, the herd turns to flee. You are caught in their path. Stampeding feet crash all around you. One lands on your leg. Bones shatter under the mammoth's weight. Then another foot lands on your chest, crushing the life out of you.

THE END

To follow another path, turn to page 225.
To learn more about the Ice Age, turn to page 314.

As the bear takes a step closer, you instinctively step backward.

"Let's run for it," you tell your friends. "I am going to throw my berries at it, and then let's go."

Out of the corner of your eyes, you see Jayla and Mateo nod.

"Here goes nothing," you say, cocking your arm back. When you throw the bowl, you shout, "Go!"

Once you turn your back, the beast gives chase. You run as fast as you can. But you are no match for the speedy bear. It catches your heel in its mouth. You stumble to the ground, and the bear is upon you. It strikes with bone-crushing blows. One paw catches you across the head, and the blow knocks you out. You fall to the ground, never to wake again.

THE END

To follow another path, turn to page 225.
To learn more about the Ice Age, turn to page 314.

You worry what the bear might do if you make any sudden moves. It might attack if you startle it. So you try to remain calm.

"Slowly set down your bowls," you tell your friends.

Out of the corner of your eyes, you see Jayla and Mateo do as you said. The bear huffs as it sniffs the air. It probably smells what's in the bowls.

"Now calmly back away," you instruct your friends.

Each one of you takes a step back. The cave bear just watches. You take another step, and still, the bear does nothing.

"How are you doing?" you ask your friends.

"I'm about to pee my pants," Mateo says, taking another step.

Turn the page.

"Can we run yet?" Jayla asks, stepping back.

"No, not yet," you say. "Just keep walking backward."

As you continue to back away, the bear moves in to sniff the bowls. It's distracted, but you're not safe yet. The three of you keep backing away slowly until the bear is out of sight.

You go find the woman who brought you here. You do your best to tell her about the bear while Mateo stands behind you growling and raising his hands in the air. The woman looks from you to him, and you think she understands. She says something urgent to the other people. They quickly gather up everything that they had collected, and the woman leads everyone back to the village.

Once you're back, Jayla points to the cave.

"We should make a cave painting of our adventure," she says.

"But the villagers are preparing a meal with the food they have gathered," Mateo replies. "We should get something to eat."

While you think it would be cool to do a cave painting, you are also feeling hungry.

To eat with the villagers, turn the page.
To go back to the cave, turn to page 280.

You can't remember the last meal you have eaten. And even though all the villagers have is some berries and seeds, that is better than going hungry.

The woman you met earlier motions you to sit down next to the fire. Then you are each handed a bowl of food.

As you eat with your fingers, Mateo asks, "Do you think we'll ever get home?"

"I hope so," you say between mouthfuls.

"At least we have everything we need to survive with these people," Jayla says.

You spend the night with the villagers, and in the morning you help them gather food again. While you continue to wonder if you will ever return home, your focus slowly turns to doing what you need to do in order to survive.

Eventually you learn the Cro-Magnon people's ways of life and even their language. You grow into adulthood and marry. You have a few children and sometimes wonder if your memories of the future were all just a dream. You live to old age, spending the rest of your life with the Cro-Magnon people.

THE END

To follow another path, turn to page 225.
To learn more about the Ice Age, turn to page 314.

Just then, you feel a sudden shiver. The sun is setting, and the cold is creeping in. It is a reminder that you are still back in the Ice Age.

"Let's go to the cave for shelter," you say. "And it would be fun to make a cave painting."

Once in the cave, Jayla rushes over to the bowls of red and black paste on the floor. There are also brushes made of some sort of hair.

"Let's paint the cave bear," she says, as she sets to work.

You walk over and grab a bowl of paint and a brush. When you touch the wall with the brush, you feel a familiar tingle shoot up your arm.

Suddenly the air is filled with the sounds of your excited classmates, and bright lights make you squint. You spin around to see that you are back in the museum.

"We're back!" you shout.

You, Jayla, and Mateo are standing in front of the museum's cave painting display.

"Did we paint that?" Mateo asks, nodding to the images in front of you.

"I don't know," you say, looking down at the brush in your hand.

Just then, Rebecca walks up to you and grabs the bowl and brush from you.

"Be careful with those," she says. "Those are some very special artifacts."

THE END

To follow another path, turn to page 225.
To learn more about the Ice Age, turn to page 314.

CHAPTER 4

AUSTRALIA

"Let's check out the exhibit on Australia," you tell your friends.

"Yeah," replies Mateo. "It's 'the land down under!'"

You have always been interested in Australia. It has some of the world's most amazing animals, from cuddly-looking koalas to monstrous saltwater crocodiles. You can only imagine what type of amazing creatures lived there in prehistoric times.

"Isn't Australia mostly desert?" Mateo asks as he follows you. "I bet it didn't get very cold."

"I bet it did," Jayla says "It was the Ice Age. And I bet we'll see some cool animals on display."

Turn the page.

"Like that one!" you say, pointing toward an animal that looks like a giant kangaroo with a short, stubby snout.

"What about that one?" Mateo says, pointing to another exhibit that appears to be part giant wombat and part hairy hippopotamus.

Then you notice a display of ancient tools off to one side.

"Hey, let's check that out," you say to your friends.

You walk over to a glass display case. It is filled with spear tips and ax heads. Most of them look to be made out of stone. Then you notice something odd. A knife that looks like it's made out of glass sits on top of the case.

"What's that doing here?" you ask as your friends lean in to see.

You reach over to touch the tool.

"Don't touch anything!" Jayla calls.

Both she and Mateo reach out to stop you from grabbing the knife. They touch you just as you pick up the mesmerizing object. Suddenly you feel a tingle in your finger. Then a wave of energy washes over you.

One moment you are standing in the museum, surrounded by your classmates. The next, you feel the crunch of dirt under your feet. Glancing around, you are surprised to be in the middle of an enormous desert with mountains lining the distant horizon.

"Whoa, what just happened?" you ask. "It looks like we're actually in Australia."

"I think we are," Jayla responds. "And I think it's the Ice Age!"

Turn the page.

"No way!" Mateo cries. "How do we get back to the museum?"

"We should probably figure that out," you say.

You and your friends are in a desert, which seems like the best place to be during an ice age. Deserts are warm, you think. But will you be safe here in a wide-open area? Who knows what sort of prehistoric creatures might be roaming about. There is a mountain range off in the distance. You might find shelter there.

To explore the desert, go to the next page.
To head for the mountains, turn to page 291.

"Let's stick around here," you tell your friends. "We appeared in the desert, so maybe if we stay put, we'll reappear back at the museum."

To pass the time, you and your friends look around for water and food. But you don't have much luck. It is the desert, after all.

Suddenly Mateo shouts, "Hey look!"

You and Jayla spin around to see Mateo pointing at some animals off in the distance. They look like kangaroos, but they are huge. The animals are taller than you. They're stocky and have stubby snouts. They don't hop like you would expect a kangaroo to, but they hobble forward on their hind feet.

"I think those are Procoptodon," Jayla says. "There was one on display in the museum."

"Do you think they're hungry?" Mateo asks.

Turn the page.

"Don't worry," you say. "Kangaroos are herbivores."

"Even giant ones?" Mateo asks.

"More like prehistoric ones," Jayla says.

You and your friends watch the Procoptodon herd lumber along. Luckily they don't seem to notice you. You are amazed to see such animals in real life.

"We really are in Australia during the Ice Age," you mumble in awe.

"Well, it's a good thing we're in a desert," Mateo says. "At least we won't freeze here."

"That's not necessarily true," Jayla says. "Not all deserts are hot. What about the Gobi Desert in Asia? It can get freezing cold there at night."

Turn the page.

What Jayla says makes you worry if you made the right decision to stay. When the sun sets, it could get very cold. And you already know that there isn't any food and water around. Maybe following the Procoptodon would lead you to a water source. But you also remember one of the most important rules if you are lost—stay put! That makes it easier for someone to find you. But who will find you in this situation? A part of you still hopes that by staying here you will somehow end up back in the museum.

To stay put and wait to be found, turn to page 295.

To head in the direction of the Procoptodon herd, turn to page 297.

You don't want to be out in the open when night falls. You won't have any protection from whatever predators might come out then. And you're pretty sure the temperatures will plummet once the sun sets. This is the Ice Age after all, and the only thing keeping you warm right now is the sun.

"Let's head for those mountains," you say. "Maybe we can find shelter there."

You begin the trek across the desert.

As you are walking, Jayla says, "Did you know that Antarctica is actually a desert?"

"What? No way," Mateo says. "I thought deserts were hot."

"It's not about how hot an area gets," Jayla explains. "It's how little moisture it gets."

Turn the page.

"It took thousands of years for Antarctica to get covered in all that ice and snow," you add.

As you reach the foothills surrounding the mountains, you start walking through a lightly forested area. When you reach a hilltop, you hear an odd noise.

"Look!" Jayla says, pointing downhill.

There you see a couple of large birds. They easily stand taller than you, and they're stocky enough to weigh more than any of you.

"They look like huge emus," you say.

"I think they're Genyornis," Jayla says. "They're a type of prehistoric flightless bird. There was a fake one on display at the museum."

Just then, you hear Mateo's stomach grumble again.

Turn the page.

"Quiet," you say. "They might hear us."

"I can't help it! I'm hungry," Mateo says.

"I think they're herbivores," Jayla says of the birds. "So we shouldn't be in danger."

That gives you an idea. Maybe if you watch these birds eat you can figure out what plants are safe for you. At this point, you would eat almost anything.

But the sun is beginning to set. You can feel it getting colder already. Maybe you should keep your focus on finding shelter instead of food.

To focus on finding shelter, turn to page 300.
To look for food, turn to page 304.

"Don't you two remember what we learned in the survival class about getting lost?" you ask your friends.

"Yeah, you're supposed to stay put," Jayla says. "Or you might get even more lost."

"Don't forget the rule of three," Mateo adds. "We can survive three days without water and three weeks without food."

"So I guess we should be OK for a little while," Jayla says.

It is settled. You are going to stay where you are in the hopes of being found. Maybe Mr. Andrist or Rebecca will figure out what happened to you and somehow bring you home.

In the meantime, you do your best to stay calm and comfortable. You spy some dried grass and twigs. You wish you knew how to start a fire.

Turn the page.

Once the sun sets, the temperature plummets. It's not just cold, it's freezing. You and your friends huddle together for warmth. Your teeth chatter.

You hadn't expected it to get this cold. That's when you remember the other part of the rule of three—you can only survive three hours in extreme weather. And that's about how long you and your friends last before you are overcome by the cold.

THE END

To follow another path, turn to page 225.
To learn more about the Ice Age, turn to page 314.

You're pretty sure no one is going to time travel into the past to find you. And the desert could get freezing cold once the sun goes down. It's best if you find some shelter before evening.

"Let's follow the Procoptodon," you tell your friends. "Maybe they'll lead us to water or somewhere we can find shelter."

Mateo and Jayla nod in agreement. You are able to keep up with the large animals for a while. But as the desert terrain turns to grasslands, you struggle to keep pace. You lose sight of the giant kangaroos, but Mateo spots other prehistoric animals.

"Hey look!" he shouts. "It's some of those hairy hippo-like animals."

"Yeah, Diprotodon," Jayla adds. "We saw one at the museum."

Turn the page.

"They don't look like meat-eaters," you say, as you watch them munching on the brush.

Still, you keep your distance. After all, the Diprotodon are about the size of hippos. You don't want to make them angry. As you are walking around the herd, you hear them squeal and grunt excitedly. Then they all start running in your direction.

"There must be a predator coming," Jayla says.

"If it's prehistoric size, we had better get out of here too!" Mateo says.

You agree with Mateo, but which direction should you run? Do you run away from the danger with the Diprotodon? Or would it be better to get out of their way and head in another direction?

To flee with the Diprotodon, turn to page 306.
To flee in a different direction, turn to page 307.

You remember reading in a survival book the rule of three. People can survive three hours in extreme weather, three days without water, and three weeks without food. So while you are hungry, you know that food is not your biggest priority. As the sun begins to dip toward the horizon, you feel the chill in the air. Overnight, it will get freezing cold. You need to find shelter.

"Let's leave the birds alone," you say to your friends. "We need to find shelter."

"Yeah, I'm feeling chilled," Jayla says.

You continue on. The foothills soon turn into mountains. You are partially protected from the wind by the trees. You even think that perhaps you could collect some fallen branches to build a shelter. But then Mateo sees something surprising.

"Look," Mateo says, pointing toward a cave in the side of the mountain.

Out of the dark cave, you see the soft glow of a fire flickering inside. For a moment you worry about who might be in the cave. But the night's chill quickly dispels any fear.

"There are people in there," Jayla whispers.

"Let's hope they are friendly," you say as you lead your friends into the cave.

There you find a group of people sitting around a fire and eating. While they seem suspicious of you, they must see that you are cold. They wave you over to join them by the fire.

As you sit down, you notice a familiar-looking knife lying next to the fire. You and your friends exchange knowing glances.

"Its the knife from the museum!" Mateo says.

Turn the page.

"Is that what sent us back in time?" Jayla asks.

"There's only one way to find out," you say.

You all reach for the knife at the same time. Suddenly the crackling of the fire is replaced by the sounds of your classmates. Instead of sitting in a cave, you find yourself back in the museum.

"We're back!" Jayla says.

Just then, you all realize that you're still clutching the knife. Instantly, you drop it. The noise attracts Rebecca's attention. She walks over and picks up the knife in her gloved hands.

"How did this get here?" she asks. Then she looks at you with a knowing smile. "I'm glad to see it's still here—and that you are too."

THE END

To follow another path, turn to page 225.
To learn more about the Ice Age, turn to page 314.

"I have an idea," you tell your friends. "What if we follow the birds and eat whatever they eat?"

"I'd prefer a cheeseburger," Mateo jokes. "But that's probably not an option."

"It's worth a try," Jayla says.

The three of you sit quietly and watch the birds. They tear up plants with their powerful beaks. From where you are, you can't tell what plants exactly they're eating. But after a bit, they wander away.

You're about to give up your search for food when you come across a nest hidden in the grass. There is one huge egg in it. You remember seeing an ostrich egg once. This is much bigger than that. And while you are not a fan of raw egg, it will be enough to feed all three of you.

You creep toward the nest. That's when you hear a loud, threatening squawk. You look around to see one of the birds. It must have stayed behind to protect the nest. The bird rushes toward you before you have a chance to flee. It kicks you hard in the chest. You hear the snap of ribs as you fly through the air. You lose consciousness from the pain, and the bird continues its attack. You never wake again.

THE END

To follow another path, turn to page 225.
To learn more about the Ice Age, turn to page 314.

"If they're running this way to get away from something," you say, "then we should too."

You and your friends take off running, but the Diprotodon quickly overtake you. Mateo shouts as he is knocked to the ground by one of the beasts. You stop to help him to his feet. As you yank him up, the grass parts in front of you. You come face to face with what looks like a giant crocodile.

It must be longer than a minivan! you think.

It rushes forward on its long legs. You are not quick enough to escape its crushing jaws.

The Diprotodon herd was fleeing from a Quinkana, a prehistoric crocodile that hunted on land. You just became its next meal.

THE END

To follow another path, turn to page 225.
To learn more about the Ice Age, turn to page 314.

You're pretty sure the Diprotodon can run faster than you. You don't want to get trampled by them.

"Let's get out of their way!" you shout to your friends.

You dart to the side of the stampeding herd as the large Diprotodon race past. The speed of the large creatures astonishes you. But they're not the only speedy animals. Right behind them, you see a large, scaly body on long legs. It has a long snout and a large mouth full of sharp teeth.

"Get down before it sees us," you call to your friends.

You all duck out of sight in the tall grass just in time.

"That lizard must have been as long as my mom's minivan," Mateo says.

Turn the page.

"It wasn't a lizard," Jayla says. "It was a Quinkana—a crocodile that hunted on land."

"What if there are more? Let's get out of here," you say.

You head in the opposite direction, away from the Quinkana. At one point, you come across a small stream. You follow it and are surprised to come upon a small village of people.

"They must be early native people," Jayla says.

You watch them from a safe distance. They have shelters, food, and fire—everything that you need to survive.

"Should we approach them?" Jayla asks.

"It's worth the risk if we want to survive," you say. "What other options do we have—to keep wandering out here and die of starvation or some horrible animal attack?"

Turn the page.

You lead your friends into the village.
The people watch suspiciously as you walk over
to a fire and sit down next to it. A woman and
a man walk over to you. The man looks angry,
but the woman puts her arm in front of him as
if to calm him down. The woman makes hand
gestures to her mouth.

"She wants to know if we're hungry," you say.

"Oh yes!" Mateo says.

You notice then that the man is holding a
familiar-looking knife. Satisfied that you mean
the people no harm, he sets it down nearby.
You and your friends make eye contact.

"Should we touch it?" Jayla asks.

"Maybe the knife is the key to getting back to
the museum," Mateo adds.

"It couldn't hurt to try," you say.

The three of you reach out quickly and touch the knife. As you do, you feel a tingle in your fingers, and then a wave of energy washes over you. Suddenly the sounds of the crackling fire are replaced by that of your excited classmates. Instead of sitting next to a fire, you find yourself standing next to the glass case.

"Whoa, we're back," Mateo says.

Just then, Rebecca walks up to you and your friends. With gloved hands, she picks up the tool sitting on top of the case.

"I've been looking for that," she says. "This quartz knife is one of those special artifacts I was talking about."

Rebecca winks at you as she walks away.

THE END

To follow another path, turn to page 225.
To learn more about the Ice Age, turn to page 314.

CHAPTER 5

THE ICE AGES

Earth's climate naturally goes through cycles of warm and cool periods. Scientists are not exactly sure why. It could be caused by changes in Earth's movement around the sun or changes in the sun itself. Large meteorite impacts, volcanic activity, and animal activity are other possible causes. There have been times in Earth's past when it has been so warm that the polar ice caps melted. There have also been times when it has been so cold that much of the planet was covered in ice and snow.

An extended period in which temperatures drop is known as an ice age. During ice ages, snow might not melt because summers are cooler, and glaciers expand to cover large areas of land.

There have been several major ice ages throughout Earth's history. The first was the Huronian Ice Age, which happened more than 2 billion years ago. Next was the Cryogenian Ice Age. It began about 850 million years ago. The Andean-Saharan Ice Age was about 450 million years ago, and the Karoo Ice Age about 360 million years ago.

Earth is actually in the middle of a fifth major ice age, which began about 2.5 million years ago. It is called the Quaternary Ice Age. It is known for having had several cooling periods during which glaciers expanded, and then warming periods, in which they retreated. These periods last for tens of thousands of years. The last glacial period began about 100,000 years ago and ended about 12,000 years ago. Currently, our planet is in the midst of an interglacial, or warm, period.

During the last glacial period, average temperatures plummeted by about 18 degrees Fahrenheit. With this extreme cooling, glaciers expanded to cover large areas of Antarctica, North and South America, Europe, and Asia.

But ice ages affect the planet in ways other than just covering areas in glaciers. As glaciers creep forward, their sheer size and weight reshapes the surface of the planet. They can carve out valleys and lakes and scrape hills from the landscape. Then when glaciers melt, they fill lakes with water, and the dirt and rock they bulldozed up gets left behind in hills.

Ice ages affect plants and animals too. The Andean-Saharan Ice Age caused Earth's first mass extinction. As the planet cooled over millions of years, about 86 percent of all plant and animal life died out.

Another mass extinction happened during the Karoo Ice Age. Nearly 75 percent of plant and animal species died out.

During the last glacial period of the Quaternary Ice Age many large animals such as the woolly mammoth, cave bear, and saber-toothed cat died out. But smaller animals that could more easily adapt to the colder climate were able to survive. Birds migrated to warmer locations.

Humans also adapted to the changing climate. They relocated to escape the bitter cold. They built shelters and used fire to keep warm. Humans also made tools to help them hunt when food was scarce. Since the last glacial period, humans have become the most dominant species on the planet.

lagoon (luh-GOON)—a shallow area of water between the coast and a coral reef that's offshore

megafauna (MEG-uh-fawn-uh)—large animals that lived around the time of the Ice Age

omnivore (OM-nuh-vor)—an animal that eats both plants and other animals

Pangaea (pan-JEE-uh)—a landmass believed to have once connected all Earth's continents together

predator (PRED-uh-tur)—an animal that hunts other animals for food

prehistoric (pree-hi-STOR-ik)—from a time before history was recorded

prey (PRAY)—an animal hunted by another animal

ray (RAY)—a type of fish with a flat body, winglike fins, and a whiplike tail

sauropod (SORE-oh-pod)—one of a group of dinosaurs with long necks, thick bodies, and long tails

terrarium (tuh-RER-ee-uhm)—a clear container used to raise land animals or as a display case

tundra (TUHN-druh)—a cold area where the soil under the ground is permanently frozen

SELECT BIBLIOGRAPHY

"Cretaceous Period." National Geographic.com. www. nationalgeographic.com/science/prehistoric-world/ cretaceous/>, Accessed March 20, 2019.

"Early Cretaceous Period," HowStuffWorks.com. animals. howstuffworks.com/dinosaurs/early-cretaceous-period.htm, Accessed March 19, 2019.

"Late Cretaceous Period," HowStuffWorks.com. animals. howstuffworks.com/dinosaurs/late-cretaceous-period.htm, Accessed March 19, 2019.

"The Big Five Mass Extinctions," COSMOS: The Science of Everything, cosmosmagazine.com/palaeontology/big-five-extinctions, Accessed June 24, 2019.

"When Have Ice Ages Occurred?" Illinois State Museum, iceage.museum.state.il.us/content/when-have-ice-ages-occurred, Accessed June 24, 2019.

Britannica: Jurassic Period. www.britannica.com/science/ Jurassic-Period, Accessed June 24, 2019.

Carr, Ada, "We're Due For Another Ice Age But Climate Change May Push It Back Another 100,000 Years, Researchers Say," The Weather Channel, weather.com/ news/climate/news/ice-age-climate-change-earth-glacial-interglacial-period, Accessed June 24, 2019.

Dinosaur Timeline Gallery, www.prehistory.com/timeline/ jurassic.htm, Accessed June 24, 2019.